WORK + LOVE

AN INSPIRATIONAL FABLE ABOUT FINDING PURPOSE

MICHAEL WOLSTEN

HENRY WOLSTEN

CONTENTS

For my boys, who have the hearts, desire,
and grit to live a life full of purpose.

PRAISE FOR WORK + LOVE

This little gem of a book is actually a treasure trove of information on making good decisions, preparing for your career and finding God's good will and purpose for your life. The father-son team of Michael and Henry Wolsten has created a fable that will draw you in and keep you turning the pages, even while it offers life principles from twenty years of experience on Michael's part, principles that son Henry is now applying to his own life. Work and love are what we were created for, and Work + Love will show you how to fill your life with both, to your own satisfaction and to God's glory.

~ Ann Tatlock, award-winning novelist, editor and children's book author

INTRODUCTION

I could hear the pain in his voice when one of my clients recently explained where he was at with his work relationships. With tears in his eyes he explained:

"I can't keep doing this anymore. I keep getting in my own way and I know there has to be something better for us, I just don't know how to get there."

You see, the stakes were incredibly high for him. Communication was at an all-time low, the frustration often boiled over into arguments, and even worse, he was ignoring the real conversations that needed to happen.

And the hardest part of all was knowing that the one relationship that needed the most help was with his son, who helped him run the family business. How he was leading was literally tearing his company and family apart.

After working with hundreds of Leaders as an Executive Coach, I hear this story all too often. It's one of the reasons that I wrote this book. While there is a limit to the desks that I can sit behind with clients, I knew that God was calling me to make a difference in the lives of everyday leaders. I didn't want to only save my clients tons of time, energy, and misery in the process of helping them lead a life full of purpose, but I wanted to create an experience that they could enjoy with their teams too.

When I first started writing this book, it was structured as a how-to guide. I wanted to write something for those just entering the workforce and starting their careers. My mission was to share much of what I learned over the last 20 years in business: what to do, what not to do, and how to be successful over the long term.

To be blunt, the book stank. Sure, the principles were important and personal to me, but the book was dry. I asked my wife to read it and tell me what she thought. She lovingly encouraged me to keep going and said there was something deeper and better that needed to be shared.

So I started over. I asked God what kind of book he wanted me to write and what story he wanted to tell. Any credit this work receives needs to be given to Him, the true author of our lives.

He also gave me the inspiration to write this version with my son Henry, who is just entering the workforce as a teenager. His passion and perspective are woven throughout this entire work and I am so grateful for the months we have spent together on this book.

So, if you're ready to fall in love with work again and apply the principles woven into this story to help you lead with God centered purpose, without having to read a dry, boring how-to manual, then this book is for you.

Enjoy Work + Love!

DON'T FORGET YOUR BONUS!

The power-packed resource *The Work + Love Companion Guide PDF* is included with this book. Grab your copy now!

Maybe you love fillable PDF resources, or just need some help and motivation to take action and see real results. We created the companion guide just for you! Get this printable resource sent to your inbox, print it out, and start putting your heart on paper.

Great for individuals or teams.

To get this bonus... just go here, plug in your name and email address, and you get access right away!

Scan Here

Also, before you turn that page, know that I am here for you and your team over on social media.

Follow me on LinkedIn, Facebook, Instagram or YouTube by searching @MichaelWolsten.

CHAPTER 1
WHO YOU ARE MATTERS

"One freaking credit, are you kidding me?" Chad shouted at the computer screen, standing up and knocking his chair over. The lanky 22-year-old slammed a fist on his desk, swiping his dishwater blonde hair out of his flashing brown eyes. "After four years in college, I'm short one credit?"

Mrs. Maria Benitez, his school counselor on the other end of the video call, stared calmly back at him. "Chad, I understand you're frustrated, but you need to calm down. The school got the wrong information, and now the plan that we had isn't going to—"

"I can't afford to be here any longer!" Chad made fists with his hands and held them against his temples, his frustration so palpable it made his body shake. "I can't pay my rent, I'm doing school and work full time, my credit card debt is piling up ... I just can't afford it!"

Mrs. B shook her head. "Chad, I'm sorry you're in this situation. I know you felt like you had to drop your last class because of your workload, but it was your choice."

"So what now? Huh? I just drop out?" Chad laughed, a dry, raspy sound that hurt his throat as it came out. "Everything I have and my mom's entire life's savings down the drain? And why?" He leaned over his desk, punctuating every word with a slam of his fist on the hardwood. "Because of one stupid credit!"

His chest heaving, Chad picked up his chair and sat down in it heavily, the wood creaking under his six-foot frame. After a few deep breaths, he asked quietly, "Please, Mrs. B... is there anything you can do? I need a miracle."

The room grew quiet as Mrs. B stared intently at him through the screen, pondering for a moment. A sly smile slowly crept its way across her face, and she began typing on her laptop. Chad looked up at the sounds, his eyes filled with burning questions. At long last, Mrs. B spoke. "There may be something."

Chad shot back to his feet, once again sending his chair to the ground. "There is? What is it? Anything, please!"

"There's this program-"

"Okay."

"It's called the Recreational Senior Nature Co-operative."

"Great."

"The program for Coeur d'Alene University isn't supposed to start until this fall, but for one of my students, I'll make some exceptions."

Once again retrieving his chair, Chad sat down and leaned forward eagerly. "What do I have to do?"

"Hiking."

Chad's spirits dropped a bit. *I hate hiking.*

"There's this friend of mine: Paul is his name. He has a leg injury that requires him to walk with a cane."

"This guy hikes?"

"He's retired, and it's what he enjoys the most. He needs a companion, other than his dog, to help him along."

"Let me get this straight," Chad said, making a church-and-steeple with his hands. "You want me to take this guy hiking up and down a hill, so that he doesn't die on the trail."

"Cut it out, Chad, it's not like that. The outreach program would take twelve weeks to complete—"

Twelve weeks!

"On Saturdays from six a.m. to one p.m—"

"You've got to be kidding me!" Chad interrupted. "Saturday is my only day off! I work all day on Sunday! Don't do this to me."

Mrs. B's gaze hardened, and her speech slowed. "I'm not doing this to you, Chad, I'm doing it for you. You're already signed up for full-time credits this summer, and all the other courses are full. Take it or leave it: this is the only way to get one more approved credit and graduate by the end of the summer. It's up to you."

Chad groaned and leaned back in his chair, his eyes closed. After a long sigh, he said, "All right ... Where do I meet this guy?"

"And you're actually doing this? Chadwick, that's great!"

Chad sighed, then immediately regretted it as the stench of week-old restaurant aprons enveloped him. WeSort4U was a commercial laundry service spanning thirteen western states. Realizing he couldn't live off his student loans and credit cards, Chad had started working there two months prior as a laundry sorter. Now, for the hundredth time, he was wishing he'd gotten a job flipping burgers instead. *I hate Fridays.*

"Yes, Mom, I want to get out as fast as possible, and if that means dragging an old timer around a mountain, so be it," Chad said, his voice traveling through his earbuds to his mother on the other end.

"Oh, Chadwick, you don't have to see it that way," she responded in a correcting tone.

"You're right, sorry: if that means dragging an old timer and his dog around a mountain, so be it."

A combination of laughter and sigh greeted his ears.

"What am I going to do with you? You know Portland is only a six-hour drive from CDA. Don't make me come out there and—"

His mom's words were cut short as Chad's left earbud was ripped out by an unwelcome hand. He jerked his head up to see his least favorite person in the world: Micah Patrick.

"Aw, is the Chaddy-baby whining to his mommy?" Micah dragged the word mommy out to three syllables. Then he put his mouth to the earbud and whined: "Oh, Mommy, life is so unfair, boo hoo hoo."

Chad shot to his feet, yanked the earbud out of Micah's hand, and pushed the grease-stained apron he was holding into the boy's smug face.

At five-foot-four, Micah wasn't particularly intimidating, but what he lacked in height, he made up for in muscle. So when Gary, the manager of WeSort4U Laundry, came around the corner to see Chad standing over the shorter man with the apron in his face, his response was not as gracious as Chad would've liked.

"Chad!" he shouted, "stop that!"

Chad dropped the apron as Gary asked, "What's going on here?"

"Chad was trying to get me to sort his sack, sir," Micah said before Chad could get a word out. "I said no, and then he shoved the apron in my face!"

"Chad," Gary said, his tone condescending, "I know this is your first job, and you don't have a lot of experience, but we do not tolerate that kind of behavior here." Unlike Micah, Gary did have the height to be intimidating, being six-foot-three of solid muscle.

"Sir, that's not—"

Gary held up his hand. "I don't want any excuses. I think you should sort Micah's sack for him to make up for this."

Micah shot Chad a look only he could see, his eyes drooping and his lower lip extended in a pout.

Chad gritted his teeth and mumbled, "Yes, sir."

"Very good. Now, Micah, come with me."

Shooting Chad one more look, Micah sauntered after Gary, leaving Chad clenching and unclenching his fists at the unfairness. For a company so large, this wasn't what he imagined when he started. *I hate this job.*

Later that night, Chad was still fuming. After having to stay an hour and a half later than normal to sort Micah's sack, he had come back to the apartment only to be reminded of the mountain of statistics homework waiting for him. *I doubt there's anything more useless I could be doing with my time,* he thought, bent over a paper with probability distributions and standard deviation problems he couldn't begin to understand.

What do statistics have to do with my degree in business management, anyway?

Chad thought back to his statistics class earlier in the week where he met a fellow student named Aiden. Aiden had the look of a tech genius, unkempt brown hair spilling over into his square-framed glasses. The two had commiserated over how awful their class was and swapped phone numbers, determining to talk later on.

After a few hours of frustration, a quick glance at the clock told him it was one a.m. He snatched the clock off the desk and stared at it.

You've got to be kidding me, he thought. *I have to be hiking with the old man in five hours.*

Slamming the clock back down on the desk so hard it hurt his hand, Chad turned and shut off his desk lamp and got into bed. He shifted, trying to get comfortable as his feet hung off the end. *I hate school.*

Chad's alarm awoke him from his dreamless sleep at five forty-five a.m. *Oh no, I must've hit snooze!*

Leaping out of bed, Chad pulled on his jeans and a shirt, put on his jacket and slipped on his loafers before racing out the door. He jumped in his little blue, late model Honda. It wasn't much to look at, with its years of abuse, but it was reliable. He slammed it into gear, and headed toward the trailhead. As he drove, the first golden rays of sunlight streamed over the hills and lit his face, basking his car in warmth despite the chill of the mid-May morning. He breathed in, allowing the daylight to wake him up a bit.

I haven't been up with the sun in so long …

He parked his car and ran toward the entrance for Tubb's Hill. Even in his mad dash, he couldn't help but admire the beauty of Lake Coeur d'Alene, the fresh smell of the pine trees, and the quiet song of birds calling to each other. He looked around frantically, but there was no one in sight. He slapped his leg in frustration. *I'm too late!*

Just as he was turning back, he heard the bark of a dog from farther along the trail. Chad's head snapped up, and he dashed down the rocky path. It was then that he realized he had forgotten to wear his tennis shoes. *Now I'm going to feel every rock on this trail.*

He rounded a corner to find a man walking with a cane and leading a Bernese Mountain dog on a leash. Its white belly extended up to its nose, and provided a striking contrast with the rest of its brown and black body. Chad reached the pair and stopped, panting, his hands on his knees.

The older man paused, looking down at him. Chad thought he looked to be in his sixties, with a six-foot-four, slightly hunched frame that testified to his many years of activity. Paul's high cheekbones and square jaw gave him the look of a tougher man, but his deep set dark blue eyes conveyed the opposite: compassion, and at the moment, amusement.

"Ah, you must be Chad. Maria told me you'd be meeting me today." His deep voice filled the forest.

Chad cocked his head. "Who?"

"You'd know her as Mrs. B," Paul said with a smile.

Indignation rose up in Chad. Filling his chest with air, he said, "Why didn't you wait for me? You're supposed to have a companion out here."

Paul's smile-wrinkles folded in on themselves as he grinned at Chad. "Early risers win the day, Chad, early risers win the day. As for my companion ..." he chuckled, "he's always with me, wherever I go."

Chad looked down at the dog, who had his tongue out, panting. Poor old man must mean his dog.

"So," Paul said, eyebrows raised. "Have you ever hiked Tubbs before?"

"Once or twice," Chad remarked offhandedly. "Honestly, I don't like hiking. I'm just doing it to get out of college."

"I love hiking; it's when I feel closest to God."

Chad scoffed, hoping Paul wouldn't notice. "Oh ... that's great. So how long is this going to take?"

"This hike, or for us to talk about why you're really here?"

"Really? Fine. I've been working my butt off in school, and I'm still one credit short of graduation, so my school counselor, Mrs.B, hooked me up with this gig, hiking with you for twelve weeks. Once that's done, well ... I'll be out, and I can do my own thing."

"That's nice, Chad," Paul said, nodding his head. "But that's not what I asked. Let me rephrase: Who are you, and why are you here?"

Chad was taken aback. "Uh, I feel like we're getting pretty personal for our first meeting."

"I'm sorry that I'm being so direct with you, Chad, but we only have twelve weeks together, so there's not a moment to lose."

What does that mean? Chad thought. "Well, I guess I'm a student and a laundry sorter. I know, super glamorous, right?"

"Okay, well, let's just say for a moment that you're out of school and not working there anymore; who would you be then?"

"I'm ... I'm not sure," Chad said with a bit of defensiveness.

There was a moment of silence, then Paul said, "Come, Chad, let's get started while the day's still young," and motioning with his hand, he set off down the trail. Chad followed, walking at a brisk pace. Despite being the younger man, he was still having a hard time keeping up. *How can he be so fast with a leg injury?*

"So, what are you getting your degree in?"

"Uh, business management," Chad shrugged.

"Why is that?"

"Well, I guess because it's easy. Plus people will hire you if you have a degree," Chad said.

Paul cocked his head. "Any thoughts on what you want to do once you have your degree?"

"... No."

Feeling irritated, Chad wrinkled up his nose. "Since we're asking questions, here's one for you: How come you hike so much if it's so hard for you?" Looking over, Paul asked, "What do you mean?"

"You know, your leg."

"Oh." Paul offered a small smile, tapping his leg as he walked. "The doctors tell me that my leg will never be a hundred percent again, and that I'll have to wear this metal contraption whenever I walk someplace. But I'm not about to let a little thing like this limit me. Life's challenges are too big for that."

Chad shook his head, feeling amazement and a small amount of guilt. He decided to ask the old man questions to get the focus off himself.

"So...what got you into hiking?"

"I used to go hiking with my father when I was a young boy," Paul replied, leaning on a tree and using his cane to climb up a steep part of the trail. "He was my first hiking companion. What about your father, Chad?"

Um, no, Chad thought. *I am not going there.*

Ignoring the question, Chad asked, "What's your dog's name?" "Grace," Paul said, reaching down and scratching the dog's ear, to its obvious delight.

They lapsed into a lengthy silence and, despite his best efforts, Chad couldn't help but think about the old timer's question, "Why do you exist?" It rang in his ears, filling his thoughts. *Why do I exist? What is my purpose?*

At around the halfway point of the hike, Chad couldn't take it any longer.

"So your question from earlier," Chad said. "I have to be honest. I don't know the answer. But let me ask you: Why are you here? Why do you exist?"

"Well, Chad, first off I don't want you to feel bad you don't know the answer to the question. To be honest, there are so many people out there who don't know who they are, and thus don't know where they're going. This is the first principle we have gone over together: **Who You Are Matters.**"

This answer put Chad at ease a bit, but the question still gnawed at him as Paul continued. "As for me, it's taken me many years to discover who I am, and why I'm here. I am loved and created by God, he gives me purpose, and as I start living that, I exist to motivate and encourage others to see who they are in God and to be operating in love in their careers."

"Huh. Wow."

"If you don't know who you are," Paul continued, "it makes it a lot harder to know where you're going. For example, because my father taught me how to hike, how to prepare, and to have a healthy fear and respect for nature, it prepared me for hiking bigger and more dangerous trails. But if I didn't know all that, I would be totally lost. The same is true for life. If we don't have any preparation, as most people don't, we can easily get lost on the trail, following paths that we probably shouldn't go on."

Who is this guy? Chad thought, taking a moment to assess what he was thinking and feeling. He sensed a mixture of anger, uncertainty, and if he was being honest, curiosity at what Paul had to say. Chad had definitely never heard anyone speak with such confidence and love before, except maybe his mom.

"Well, it looks like we survived our first hike together." Paul's voice invaded his thoughts.

Chad, who'd been looking at the trail beneath his feet, snapped his head up to discover they were back at the trailhead where they started.

"Wow," he said. "How far did we go today?"

"About four miles," Paul replied, scratching Grace's side. "Chad, thanks for hiking with me today. I know we covered a lot more ground than you were planning on, both on the trail and our conversation. Will you do me a favor and think some of what we talked about? We can discuss what you discover next week."

"Um ... sure," Chad said, giving him a half shrug. *Whatever.*

"All right then, see you next Saturday." With that, Paul and Grace walked to the parking lot, out of sight behind a wall of trees.

What an odd old man, Chad thought.

CHAPTER 2
THE HAND YOU'VE BEEN DEALT

C had had one of the worst nights of sleep in his life after his conversation with Paul. He kept tossing and turning, trying to get comfortable, two questions reverberating through his thoughts: *Who am I? Why do I exist?*

With almost no rest he was exhausted, both mentally and physically. He couldn't remember the last time he had traversed four miles, especially not on a hike. So he was in no condition to put up with Micah's antics the next morning as they unloaded a shipment of shop rags from a semi-truck parked at the loading bay. Chad had his arms full with a sack dripping with grease, which is why he didn't see Micah's foot sticking out in front of him. Tripping over it, Chad went down hard, skinning his elbows on the rough pavement. The rags spilled out of the sack, littering the floor.

Rising to his knees, Chad glared at Micah, who mockingly offered his hand to help Chad up. Chad, rising to his feet, smacked away Micah's hand. The bubbling vat of anger inside him threatened to overtake him and end his short-lived career at WeSort4U Laundry. Suddenly, a thought entered his mind: *Who am I? Who will I be if I hit Micah?*

He didn't like the answer: he'd get fired for sure, and with no paycheck he would have to drop out of college. Chad shook his head, trying to clear it, but the thought remained. He turned away, gathering up the spilled rags, and headed back inside, all the while wondering, *What just happened?*

As the week progressed, Chad continued to wrestle with the questions swirling around his mind. He realized how many questions he had about so many different things, and was surprised at how few answers he had: *How do I deal with Micah? Why does he do these things? What happens when I finish school? Can I keep up this pace for the next eleven weeks? Do I have a plan?* The conflict seemed to come to a head that Wednesday night, as he toiled away over the questions for the upcoming statistics test.

Even his living conditions frustrated him: a sparsely decorated studio apartment with a small desk crammed up against a wall. One framed picture of him and his mom on vacation, the only break from the dull brown wood.

His phone buzzed in his pocket. Welcoming the reprieve, Chad opened the message. Aiden, from statistics class, had texted: *Hey, Chad, I got the answer key to the test tomorrow. You want in?*

Breathing out slowly, Chad put the phone down. He had been worried about how well he would do, and this answer key would be sure to give him an A, but he had never cheated on anything before.

What does it matter? one part of him thought. *If Aiden and his friends are doing it, what's wrong with getting in on the action?*

He was about to pick up the phone and respond when the same thoughts that had been plaguing him all week returned in full force: *Who am I? Who will I be if I cheat? Will I really earn my degree?*

Chad silently chided himself, feeling he was being stupid, but there was something inside him that just wouldn't let him pick up the phone. He groaned, putting his hand on his face as he leaned back in his chair.

CHAPTER 3
HOW YOU SEE THE WORLD SHAPES YOU

C had was determined not to have a repeat of the last hike, so on Saturday morning he got up at his alarm, put on his tennis shoes, and got to the Mineral Ridge Trailhead five minutes early. He recognized the vintage, cherry red pickup truck Paul rode in and was dismayed. *Please don't let me be late again.*

He was relieved to find Paul and Grace at the trailhead map, Paul tracing his fingers along the route Chad supposed they'd be following.

"Good morning," Paul said, his deep voice bringing Chad a small amount of comfort.

"Morning."

"I'll be honest, Chad," Paul said, leaning against his cane and staring into Chad's eyes. "I've been thinking about you all week. I'm looking forward to today, but I must warn you, it will be a bit more difficult than last time."

"The hike?" Chad asked, cocking his head to the side.

Paul nodded. "The hike ... and the conversation."

Chad felt a mixture of anxiousness and excitement. He didn't know where they were going, both in the hike and the conversation, but he knew he couldn't stay where he was, so he followed Paul down the path and into the towering arms of the trees. After a short distance, Paul said,

"So, Chad, tell me about your week. I'm sure you have lots of thoughts swirling around your head."

Chad was aware that the tension was rising up within him, but he tried his best not to let it show. "Of course I have thoughts! You, like, Jedi mind tricked me into questioning everything I do and say! I don't know how to think anymore!"

Chad's voice carried farther than he intended it to. Paul chuckled, then waved his hand in front of Chad, saying, "These aren't the droids you're looking for."

"You know what I mean!"

"Chad, one of my favorite speakers, Dan Mohler, says, 'When you look at people through God's eyes, through His lens, you see other people the way that He sees them.' By that he means the posture and position of your heart, and knowing who you are and whose you are, changes everything. This brings us to our second principle: **How You See the World Shapes You.**"

Chad threw his hands up in the air, abandoning all politeness. "I don't know where to start. You've asked me who I am. I'm a student, but a student who hates school, who's so focused on getting by that I'm willing to consider cutting corners and do whatever it takes to get it done!"

"I can understand why you'd be feeling overwhelmed. Can I ask you: what do you think got you to where you are now?"

"Honestly? I don't know ... I feel like, 'Who cares?' you know? As long as I do what I need to and get to move on in my life, especially with school and my crappy job, what does it matter if I cheat on a test or don't fold some stinking laundry? I'm so done with all of it. Outside of you and my mom, nobody cares who I am, only what I can do for them."

"Hmm ... Chad, can I tell you a story?" Paul asked, gazing at him with caring eyes.

Chad shrugged and said, "Sure, anything to get my mind off my legs burning. This hike is way harder than last time."

Paul smiled at Chad's remark before saying, "Back when I was your age, a group of us college friends would go camping in Eastern Oregon every Memorial Day weekend. Have you ever been to Eastern Oregon before?"

Chad shook his head.

"Well, the area where we camped had rolling hills, but was dry and included lots of sagebrush, where few trees dotted the landscape. The only real town was forty-five minutes away, so we were in total isolation. The rugged terrain captivated me, and so I left camp one evening in search of the perfect sunset."

Paul and Grace stopped walking, and the older man began using his cane to start drawing some diagrams in the dirt.

"I told a few guys where I was going and then headed west from camp. I wanted to get a good view of the burning red sun, so I ventured out a bit farther than I was first planning. I broke some branches on bushes along the way, so I could find my way back fairly easily.

"I watched the sunset longer than I intended. I got wrapped up in nature and the beauty of what God creates for us to enjoy. But when I started to head back, I found only a few of the branches I had broken along the way, and I couldn't find my original trail. I doubled back and tried again, but to no avail.

"It started getting dark and a quiet panic started setting in. *What if they don't find me out here before sunset?* I thought. So I did what many of us do when we can't find the right path: I decided to go my own way.

"I thought I had a good idea of where I was and the direction I needed to go, so I stopped looking for my broken tree branches and tried to fast-walk back to camp.

"But with no guide or direction, what I thought was due east back to camp ended up being a diagonal, almost ninety-degree route that led me past the camp and back out to the road we came in on."

Paul drew a few more lines in the dirt to illustrate his point.

"When I saw the road, my heart sank. I knew I had made a mistake, because now not only was I on a road on the opposite side of camp, I had no idea where we had turned off the main road when we first came in. I was in the middle of the Oregon wilderness. The night was fast approaching, and I was lost.

"At that point it was a matter of finding the right path back to camp, and fast. So I started praying and asking God to help me find the entry point from the main road. I started walking up and down quickly, then a light jog, and then full-on running up and down the road, looking for the entry point before I started losing daylight. As dusk was settling in, a few realizations came to me.

"I was alone. I only had God to comfort and guide me from this point forward. Everything else I had tried had failed miserably.

"Everyone was looking for me in the complete opposite direction, miles away, because I had decided to go my own way. This put me even farther outside of where they could look or think of looking.

"Coyotes come out at night, and a pack of them started howling as dusk turned to night.

"I was genuinely afraid for my life. I started thinking about how I could try to find a place of shelter on the side of the road and try to fight off any coyotes. To say I was at a crisis point would be an understatement."

"Wow," Chad said, putting his hand on his forehead. "That sounds rough. What happened?"

Paul shrugged and said sadly, "The coyotes got me in the end."

Chad rolled his eyes. "C'mon, what really happened?"

Paul offered a small smile as he continued, "I was scared and could only think of one solution: crying out for help. So that's what I did. I started yelling, 'I'm on the road!' over and over again, as I ran back and forth.

"I didn't know where our camp was, I didn't know where my friends were, but I knew if I had any hope of them finding me, I needed to yell for help, as loudly as I could. I ran up and down that road, yelling for the next forty minutes or so.

"I thought about giving up. I was too far away from camp. They would never hear me from where I was. As my voice started to get hoarse from shouting, I began to question myself. Was I sealing my fate of being eaten by yelling, letting every predator know where I was?

"But as darkness surrounded me, I saw something incredible ... Headlights!"

Chad gasped, invested in the story. "They found you?"

Paul nodded. "They did. Many of my friends had been searching in the opposite direction from where I was, where I had started this whole adventure. But luckily for me, some of them had stayed behind at camp to keep an eye on things and they had heard my faint cry.

"They had been praying that I would return safely to camp and were confused when they heard a cry that did not sound like a coyote, coming from the direction of the road. So two of them decided to hop in a pickup truck and drive out to see if it could possibly be me. They found me and brought me back to safety.

"My excitement at getting back to camp was filled with the realization that I could have died out there, and that a relaxing evening, meant for fellowship and connection, had turned into a stressful search-and-rescue mission. I was ashamed and apologized to the entire group for my actions. Choosing my own path had consequences, not only for me, but for those around me as well."

Paul cocked his head to one side. "Do you understand why I'm telling you this, Chad?"

"Not really, no."

"You see, the reason I told you that story is to show that I was the one who chose the wrong path. There were clear markers along the way that showed me where I should've been going, but instead of following them, I put myself in a life-threatening position. I fear with what you're telling me, you may be on the wrong path, like I was."

Chad's awe at the story melted away and was replaced with offense at the perceived insult. "How can you say I don't care, or I'm doing it wrong? I'm killing myself doing work and school! I'm doing my best!"

Paul nodded, resuming the hike as Chad stomped beside him. "If you're giving your best, then why are you struggling with cheating and with your relationships at work?"

Chad's mouth dropped open, and he was about to come back with a biting comment when Paul continued, "I know that may sound harsh, but I want you to see that what you're saying and what you're doing aren't matching up, and it's creating a crisis inside of you. And unfortunately, Chad, it's not only you, but millions of others on this planet who struggle with finding the right path."

Chad took several deep breaths, trying to calm down as he realized Paul was trying to paint a broader picture for him.

CHAPTER 4
CHOOSING A DIFFERENT PATH

"Let me bring it to you this way," Paul said. "It actually emphasizes our third principle: **Choosing a Different Path.** Have you heard anyone, at school or work, make the following statements:

I just need to work until I can retire, or win the lottery.

I'm just a (fill in the blank); I don't have a lot to offer.

I'm only going to be as loyal to my employer as they are to me.

"Do any of those ring a bell?"

Chad thought for a moment, then nodded his head. "Yeah, they sound familiar."

Paul smiled. "Good. Now we're going to use a bit of math to help us look deeper into these statements."

Chad groaned. "As long as it's not statistics."

"No, I'm not that cruel." Paul chuckled. "We're going to take the word Work and use it to represent a lot of what we've been talking about. This includes school, your current job, and your future career."

"All right."

"Now we're going to add one of these statements to it and see what we get. Our first example: let's take work plus the statement 'I need to work until I can retire, or win the lottery.' What does that sound like to you?"

"Well, it doesn't sound super exciting when you put it that way," Chad said, rubbing the back of his neck.

"You're right, it doesn't. The word I'd use for that statement and others like it is *Apathy*. Webster's 1828 Dictionary describes it as 'Want of feeling, incapable of being stirred by pleasure, pain, or passion.' Who wants to live like that?"

"Yeah, I know some people who live that way," Chad said, shrugging.

"You're right, Chad, there are a lot of folks who live that way. I want you to consider if you," Paul said, inclining his head, "have some of those same thoughts."

Chad opened his mouth, then closed it, considering within himself for a moment. "So, you mean I can be working toward something," he asked, "but I can lack passion and purpose in it? And if I am, it's purposeless because, like you said, I'm 'want of feeling'?"

"Want of feeling is the best case scenario here," Paul said. "What this often leads to is growing contempt inside you toward work and life. This leads to frustration, which leads to anger and even hatred for the thing we're doing, and the people who are surrounding our life. Do you see what I'm saying here, Chad?"

Oh my gosh, Chad thought, his eyes widening, *I've been pouring my blood, sweat, and tears into school and work, but I'm not enjoying or finding any purpose in it. What started out as excitement, a new job and a new school, has turned into–*

Chad's thoughts were interrupted by Grace, who barked at a squirrel as it raced up a tree on the side of the trail.

"Chad, as you're contemplating this specific area for your own life, let's go back to our equation, Work plus Apathy, which is going to equal something we'll call X for now. We'll get to what X is in a moment, but for now let's take a look at our questions from another angle."

Chad nodded, still pondering his purpose.

"Let's take this statement we heard a moment ago, which is 'I'm only a (fill in the blank); I don't have a lot to offer.' Now, do you remember what you said on our first hike, when I asked you who you were?"

Chad's heart grew heavy as he responded, "I said, 'I'm only a laundry sorter.'"

Paul nodded. "What did that comment mean to you?"

"It means what I do, and who I am, doesn't add up to much at the moment ... which is why I'm going to school, so I can be more and offer something to the world. Right now, though, I'm... not."

"For me the word for that is *Self-pity*," Paul said. "I want to help you see that if you don't know who you are, and have the character built up you need, you'll always view your value and worth in work from a negative point of view. I believe our status and position has to do with our relationship with God and others first, and when that's securely in place, we won't tie our work into who we aren't and what we're lacking, but who we are and what we can bring."

"So when I'm saying I'm just a student, or when I'm saying I can't do something, I'm coming from a place of self-pity? Sounds pretty harsh to me."

"I'm trying to help you see how apathy twists the excitement and purpose work brings us, self-pity turns us inward instead of outward. I think self-pity robs us and others of being able to give our best. The thoughts of 'woe is me' and 'I'm not good enough' drown out the potential and drive inside us, crippling us from the beginning."

"So...Work plus Self-Pity equals X too?" Chad asked, "What is X again?"

"I promise we'll get there, Chad. What we're talking about together today is a path few walk on, and one that took me over thirty years of success and mistakes to fully pursue."

As he said this, Paul and Chad reached the lookout at the end of the trail. Instead of walking to the main platform, Paul turned off the trail and worked his way down to a shallow ditch that ran about five feet below the lookout. Chad followed, realizing Paul was leading him to a flat area, pointing a different direction than the main trail, and revealing a different angle other hikers didn't normally see.

The view was breathtaking: an open expanse that revealed the true scale of Lake Coeur d'Alene, the clear blue of the water enhancing the green of the pine framing the lake. To the west, the buildings of downtown Coeur d'Alene clustered around the beach, as if they too were spectators gazing in awe at the sheer scope of nature.

"Our final equation," Paul said, gazing out at the landscape before him, "is one that focuses on what we think we deserve. Remember the statement, 'I'm only going to be as loyal to my employer as they are to me.' What does that sound like to you?"

"I mean," Chad said, "it kinda makes sense. If I put in good work, I need to make sure I get something back from the company, or my school, in return."

Paul remained silent, so Chad continued. "I mean, even when they've done me wrong, like making me do one extra credit when it was their fault, the least they can do is help me make sure I don't go broke before the summer ends ... right?"

Paul opened his mouth to respond, but Chad could feel the angst inside him coming out, and felt the need to keep releasing it. "And don't get me started about work! I've only been there a few months and I've already had to put up with so much junk from Micah, not to mention handling someone's week-old food aprons, and on top of the crazy swing-shift hours! Like, who thought it was a good idea to sort clothes in the middle of the night? The whole thing is ridiculous."

Paul cocked his head, looking at Chad as he breathed heavily from his tirade. "Chad, I can see there are definitely frustrations with your work and school. It sounds like you're looking at these two areas with an attitude of *Entitlement*, and that directly ties into the statement we looked at earlier. Entitlement lifts up our efforts, and focuses only on what we're doing and what we're not getting in return."

"Hold on," Chad said, "I'm only being rational here. Why would I want to give out effort, and work harder, for someone or something without making sure I get what I deserve?"

"That's one of the biggest paradoxes in life. The more we work and serve, giving of ourselves sacrificially, the more we gain in ways we would never expect, above and beyond anything we could imagine: emotionally, physically, and spiritually. When we do this, our wants and needs from others become more of an afterthought than the main thought. I want to talk more about this, but for the sake of today, let's go back to our equation."

Chad's head was spinning. He felt the war inside him intensifying; his head was telling him not to listen to what Paul was saying, while his heart was begging him to take heed.

"To me, the statement we just looked at is full of entitlement. The focus on what I think I need and deserve. It all adds up to a lot of trouble. It's really Work plus Entitlement." Paul leaned forward on his cane, taking his gaze from the land around him and looking at Chad.

"What it comes down to is this:

Work + Apathy = X

Work + Self-Pity = X

Work + Entitlement = X

And X = Pride."

"So ... pride is bad?" Chad asked, confused. "I always thought pride was good, you know, like being proud of my mom for working multiple jobs, or something like that."

"You're right, Chad, there is a version of pride that's positive and healthy. The pride you feel for your mother is rooted in love. It's not about puffing yourself or her up, it's about seeing yourselves in the right way to begin with. The pride I'm talking about ruined my career and I almost lost my house."

"Really?" Chad asked. "How?

"Here ..." Paul walked to a small boulder and sat down on it, Grace lying down in front of him. "Let me explain. Early in my professional career, I was working for a phone book company. Have you ever seen a phone book before?"

"Yeah," Chad said, smiling. "I think I saw one in a museum once."

"Oh, come now." Paul chuckled. "I'm not that old. Anyway, I became the top salesperson in our office in just a few months. We were selling in Ontario, Oregon to help close out a book and I felt stuck. I didn't know anyone in the area and we still had the back of the book open to sell. Everyone wanted to sell the back of the book. I remember sitting in a fast food restaurant parking lot when I looked up and saw a giant billboard for the local casino and at the time I thought, *What do I have to lose by calling them?* I did, and I pitched them the back of the book. They loved it, and said yes, and I became the hero of the office.

"From that moment on, things went downhill for me, professionally and personally. You see, I bought into the lie I was hot stuff, I could sell anything, what I was doing was not lucrative enough for someone of my abilities. I made more money that year than I ever had in my entire life up to that point. So, I decided to quit."

Chad was shocked. "Why? Did you have a better job to go for?"

Paul nodded. "I sure thought so. I had an acquaintance at the time who was a successful commission-only insurance agent. I left a good job for a potential opportunity I knew very little about. I was so focused on myself and what I could do, and what I could prove to others, that I did not see how set up for failure I was. I lasted in that role all of three months and nearly lost everything. Why? I thought I was entitled to more, though I was not ready financially, mentally, or spiritually."

"So, from your story," Chad said, connecting the dots, "you felt like you didn't get what you deserved, so you felt entitled to what you thought was a better job, even though you weren't ready for it?"

"Right. I caused myself and my family so much heartache because my pride and focus on self overtook even the good things that were happening around me. You see, pride is an evil beast that will never be satisfied. You can give it your work, your whole life, your very existence, but ultimately you will be completely and utterly consumed by the devouring power of your own selfishness."

Paul let Chad ponder for a moment, then said, "Let's head back down."

As they walked the way they had come, Chad was silent, his mind reeling from everything Paul had imparted to him. Halfway back to the trailhead, Chad finally spoke.

"Paul, this all sounds pretty hopeless," he said, looking down at the trail. "I feel like giving up. What you're talking about sounds like more work, not less."

"Chad, the groundwork we're laying with what we're talking about will not only help you prevent decades of heartache for yourself, your family, and your coworkers, but will prepare you for our next equation, which is the best equation of all."

"What's that?" Chad asked, a small amount of hope rising up within him.

"It's Work + Love. It's the secret antidote to pride itself, and all the other variations of it that take us off the trail we're meant to be on."

"Work + Love," Chad said softly, rubbing his chin as he stepped over a fallen branch. "What does that equal then?"

"It actually equals lots of different things: purpose, destiny, meaning, value ... The world can take something like work, and using the power of pride, turn it into an idol of massive proportions. When you're using the power of love, you turn it into an act of service to others, and an act of worship to God. Work + Love is the most important equation in life, Chad."

Chad sighed. "Paul, honestly, I don't know how to feel about all this God stuff."

"Are you open to hearing more about the love I'm talking about? A love that surpasses understanding, feelings, and rational thinking?"

"I don't know," Chad said, "I hear the truth in what you're saying, but it's also a lot for me to take in."

"I know what we've been talking about these last two Saturdays has not been easy, but if you apply them, they can be life changing for you. Where I'd like to take us next can only happen if you're open and willing to go there. Next week we'll talk about what, and Who, love is," Paul said, looking sideways at him.

Who love is? Chad thought.

"And how the God of the universe sees you," Paul continued. "When we meet up on Saturday, if you don't want to go in that direction, I'll respect that. We can talk about sports, or the weather, for the next ten weeks instead."

Chad smirked. "I don't know if you're up to that."

Paul smiled back, but his face turned serious. "With all seriousness, Chad, there has to be a deep hunger and desire coming from you to see and do things differently for us to continue down this path. I've spent our hikes outlining the need for a vision to live differently. So moving forward, I want to extend an invitation to you: I can help you change the way you live your life and the way you do your work. I won't force it upon you ... so, if you say no, we can have a casual relationship, and by the time our hikes are done, we'll never have to speak again. The choice is yours."

Paul finished as they reached the trailhead, back where they had started. Chad smirked at the older man. "Well, I guess you've given me a lot to think about once again."

Paul smiled broadly. "Guilty as charged. You'll be in my thoughts and prayers this week, Chad. I'm looking forward to our next adventure together."

He waved his hand and turned around, and with a backwards glance, said, "Oh, by the way, if you choose to talk more about work and your life, I suggest you bring a notebook to our next hike."

With a quick call to Grace, Paul walked to his truck and climbed inside. In a few moments he was gone, leaving Chad staring at the spot where the truck had been, wondering, *What do I do now?*

CHAPTER 5
A HIGHER VISION

"Yeah, Mom, that's the thing. He basically left it up to me," Chad said into his phone. The wood of his desk chair creaked in protest as he leaned back, letting his gaze sweep his room as he talked.

"Wow, Chad," his mom's voice came through the speakers, "that's incredible. I feel like I need to talk to Paul now. It sounds like he's got so much wisdom about life and work ... about God."

Chad groaned. "C'mon, Mom. Don't start on the God stuff."

"Chadwick, just listen to me for a minute," she responded. "I ... I haven't been in touch with God for years now. I wanted to know him early on in life. I was excited about following him. But, when your father left us when you were six—"

"Mom," Chad said, his voice a bit barbed, "don't. Please."

"Let me finish ... When he left, my spiritual life took a backseat. I became so focused on just surviving day to day, and providing and giving you as much as I could, I completely forgot about God. I told myself I just didn't have time anymore for that sort of thing. I've got to tell you, Chad, my life hasn't gotten any better. It has actually gotten worse since I stopped talking to God."

Chad was shocked. "You were into that stuff?"

"Chadwick ... I lost sight of the fact that I have a Father in Heaven who loves me and cares for me, so much so I never really told you about him before, but it's true. I gave my life to Jesus at age seven, and although I've neglected and actively tried to steer clear of Christianity for so long, after eighteen years, I'm finally seeing my desperate need for God in my life."

There was a long moment of silence before Chad's mother spoke again. "The point I'm trying to make is this: listen to Paul. From what you've told me, he's very wise about life, work, and living the right way. He's a blessing from God to you, Chad. Listen to him. Receive from him. Allow him to help you change your life... give some room for thoughts about God, okay?"

Chad's mind reeled. He had no idea what to say, so he simply responded, "Okay. I gotta get to class, Mom. I love you."

"Love you too. Talk to you soon."

The three quick beeps in his ear told Chad the phone call had ended, so he set down his phone and put his head in his hands, rubbing his tired eyes with his fingertips. *What does this all mean?*

Minutes later, Chad entered his statistics classroom and took his usual spot at the back of the class. He placed his bag on the desk in front of him, resting his head on it. The exhaustion of work and school was catching up to him, and he was about to close his eyes when the door of the classroom reopened with a loud crash.

All eyes were focused on Aiden as he strutted into the room. Chad's eyes opened wide as he looked at the young man's apparel. A brand new designer watch rested on his wrist, as well as the hottest athletic shoes on his feet. He carried one of the most expensive, fastest-running laptops available in his right hand, which Chad noticed had a green snake logo on the back of the screen. He placed it on the desk next to Chad's bag as he sat down.

The teacher started his lecture, but it wasn't long at all before Chad whispered, "Dude, what happened to you?"

Aiden looked up from the notes he was taking, although it looked

26

more like a drawing to Chad. "What do you mean?"

"Last time I saw you, you were like, wearing sweatpants with holes in them. How'd you get all this stuff?" Chad asked.

Aiden chuckled, raising his watch so Chad could see it better. "Oh, you mean this. Well, I started a bit of a ... lucrative side hustle. I was able to buy all these nice toys."

"Man, what are you doing to make that kind of money?" Chad shook his head. "I mean, I don't have time to do a side hustle, but I would love to make that kind of cash. I'm having a hard enough time as it is."

"Well, I was kind of hoping you'd say that," Aiden smiled. "This business is going to need more partners as it grows, and I'm thinking you might be an excellent fit."

"What do you have going on?"

Before Aiden could answer, Professor Simmons stopped talking and glared up at the two of them. Chad gulped.

"Let's talk later," Aiden said quickly, returning to his pretend notes.

Chad tried to focus on the lecture, but his mind was caught up in what Aiden had said.

❦

The week continued, and Chad found himself more aware of his thoughts and feelings than he ever had been before. He was more readily recognizing the flashes of anger and confusion within him, even when little things came up.

His thoughts throughout the week kept returning to his father, and as much as he tried to repress them, he couldn't stop them. *Who was he? Where is he now? Does he ever think about me? What does his life look like?*

What struck him deeper, right into his core, were his thoughts about God. What his mom had said, calling him a father, disturbed him to a profound level. He realized he had always equated, without thinking about it, the word 'dad' or 'father' to his feelings of abandonment and loneliness he harbored deep inside.

He found, upon close inspection, the reason he was so angry at authority, in any form or fashion, was because he felt resentment toward the man who was supposed to be the biggest authority figure in his life: his father.

Questions constantly filled his brain, some of them even filtering into his dreams. *Why did the questions Paul asked impact my mom so much? Why is he trying to help me? Does he believe what he's saying? Is there more to my life than what I'm already doing and planning on? Is there a God? How can I be sure if I can't see him?*

On Friday evening, as he pondered what he had accomplished during the week, Chad had never felt closer to either breakthrough or breakdown. He knew that no matter what conversation he would choose for Saturday's hike, it would be a defining moment.

∼

Chad felt a mixture of nervousness and excitement as he turned off the freeway to head toward Canfield Mountain. The early sunlight and warm breeze were a reminder that June was in full swing and summer was fast approaching.

One thing Chad didn't have mixed feelings about was getting up so early. In the beginning, he had detested the interruption, but now it was one of his favorite parts of the week, being awake to smell the fresh grass, listening to the wind play through the tree branches, and watching the city awaken around him as he drove through it.

When he arrived at the trailhead, Chad saw Paul and Grace in the expanse of grass to the right of the path. Paul threw a bright yellow tennis ball, his arm propelling the object high into the sky. Grace went running after it, catching it perfectly between her teeth as she leaped into the air. Paul laughed with delight as Grace trotted back toward him, her prize secure between her jaws.

Chad watched the pair play together for another minute. He marveled at the close relationship Paul seemed to have with the animal. At length, Paul looked over and noticed Chad for the first time.

"Good morning, Chad!" Paul called out, walking toward him. Grace followed close behind, eyes still trained on the ball in Paul's hand.

"Nice weather we're having," Chad responded.

Paul's gait slowed a bit, his expression slightly somber as he nodded knowingly. "It sure is."

There was a short moment of silence when Paul reached him. Then came the words, "Well, there's no time like the present to get started. We wouldn't want to waste a beautiful morning."

Chad nodded. "That's a cool quote, let me write that down."

He reached into his pocket, pulled out a small spiral bound notebook and began to write inside with a pen.

Paul looked confused for a moment, then realization dawned as he cocked his head and narrowed his eyes. "You're pulling my leg, aren't you?"

"Yeah ... I've been thinking a lot about everything we've been talking about these past few weeks. I even talked to my mom about it," Chad said, tucking the notebook back into his pocket.

"Oh?" Paul asked as they began to walk up the trail, Grace following behind.

"Yeah, apparently she's a Christian like you."

"Apparently?" Paul asked, raising an eyebrow.

"Yeah, well, she says she stopped believing or talking to God, or whatever, when ... when something happened."

"I've heard the same story quite often, Chad. There's so many times when peoples' life and faith collide, and all that's left is confusion and separation from a real loving Father, who in his own words says he will 'never leave you or forsake you.'"

Chad sighed. "I'm sorry, Paul, I have a hard time with that because ... well, just for lots of reasons. For instance, when I was younger I remember hearing a story about Adam and Eve. And how they did one bad thing and God had to leave them and kicked them out of the garden."

"So, would it be fair to say you see God as an all-powerful judge who's just waiting for us to mess up? Waiting for a reason to leave you?" Paul asked.

"Yeah, I guess I see him as someone who does stuff to me, instead of for me, if that makes any sense."

Paul nodded. "You're not alone in that train of thought, Chad. In fact, it ties right into our fourth principle: **A Higher Vision**. So many people view what happened in the Garden in the context of their relationship with God and his intentions toward them. They view God's role in that narrative as one of disappointment and judgment, instead of seeing his love in it."

"Love? That doesn't sound very loving to me," Chad said, brow furrowed.

"Let's maybe view this from a different perspective. In Genesis 3:22, God talks about what happened after Adam and Eve decided to eat the fruit, which represented the choice of separating themselves from having a deeper relationship with God.

In that verse, God says: 'Behold, the man has become like one of us, knowing how to distinguish between good and evil, and now he might stretch out his hand and take from the tree of life as well, and eat its fruit, and live in this fallen, sinful condition forever. Therefore, God sent Adam out of the garden to till and cultivate the ground from which he was taken.'"

"Huh ... so," Chad asked, "God did that for their own good?"

"That's right, Chad," Paul said. "By sending them away, he made sure they would not be left permanently in their sin, so eventually he could once again be with them, as he had always intended."

Paul's eyes grew misty as he said, "That's the power God's love has for us: it's uniquely individual and purposeful. He desires a personal relationship with each and every one of us, above everything else, even when we choose to reject him and try to move him out of the way."

Chad and Paul had a few minutes of silence as they hiked, Chad contemplating what Paul had said.

He broke the silence. "I think I'm starting to see a side of God I haven't really been exposed to before, Paul. Can you help me with the last part though? If God is loving and wants to have a relationship with Adam, why did he make it so he had to work so hard?"

"'By the sweat of your face you will eat bread, until you return to the ground from which you were taken; for you are dust, and to dust you shall return,'" Paul quoted.

"Yeah," Chad said. "How is that loving?"

Paul nodded his head. "You're right, Chad. This verse is very sobering and tragic because it shows the weight of man's sin after the fall and what had to happen in relation to work.

"Provision was not freely given after the fall of man; it had to be earned. Man had to work the earth incredibly hard, just to put food on the table. The relationship changed from one of stewarding over the abundance in the garden to being cast out into an area where every crop and harvest was going to be full of toil and sacrifice.

"Unfortunately, many Christians have this same view of work today; they believe work is a curse put upon us by the fall of Adam. That would be true if Jesus had not come to redeem all things, including the workplace."

"I thought Jesus supposedly died for our sins," Chad said, his eyebrows raised. "Why would he care about the work we do?"

"In the Bible, we will begin to see God not only desires for us to have a higher vision for our work, but those who follow him live under a new promise, one that guarantees the same abundant life God originally intended all the way back with Adam."

"I'm confused. You say Jesus died so we wouldn't have 'toil and sacrifice' in our work, but that's what I experience every day," Chad said.

Paul explained, "In Colossians 3:22-24, it says:

'Servants, in everything, obey those who are your masters on earth, not only with external service, as those who merely please people, but with sincerity of heart because of your fear of the Lord. Whatever you do, work from the soul, as for the Lord and not for men, knowing it is from the Lord that you will receive the inheritance which is your reward. It is the Lord Christ whom you serve.'

"This verse shows us that the old way, the toil and penalty of work placed on Adam in the Old Testament, is redeemed after Christ gets involved.

"It shows servants, those that work willingly and those that work unwillingly, are able to start being redeemed in their work because they have a heart that wants to serve the Lord.

"Chad, this means employees, bosses, business owners, parents, household managers, and literally everyone else can work unto the Lord and break the curse of Genesis 3:19.

"We can live in the truth that Christ allows us to work in the Garden again with the Father and everything we do on earth now honors him when we dedicate our lives to him.

"Chad, I'm laying out this foundation for you, so you can see God's intentions for you. He cares deeply about who you are and is inviting you to walk down the path of becoming love."

"I think ..." Chad started hesitantly, "I think I need some time to think about what you've said. I do appreciate you answering my questions, and helping me see things from a different perspective. I think I've got some of the main points written down. Can I read them back to you?"

"Go ahead," Paul responded, leaning over to look at the small piece of paper in Chad's palm. "Chad, if my own experience has shown me anything, it's that as more is being revealed to you, it has the ability to bring you close to the Lord's heart," Paul said, and as he did, he placed his arm around Chad's shoulder in a loving embrace.

Chad's whole body stiffened. He couldn't remember the last time someone had hugged him, outside of his mom.

He could feel a brief struggle within his chest: one part of him felt so good to be embraced, but the other part felt years of pent up anger and resentment, and as it overcame all else, Chad shrugged off Paul's arm and quickened his pace half a step up the trail.

Paul looked at Chad kindly, his eyes portraying understanding, and the anger inside Chad came to the forefront of his mind again. *Why is he so calm?*

The rest of the hike was spent in silence as the companions followed the twisting trail through the rocky hills until they arrived back at the trailhead, Chad and Grace breathing heavily, Paul calm and collected as ever.

"I'll be thinking about you this week, Chad," Paul said, breaking the silence.

"Thanks." Chad bristled, then he turned and walked to his car, not looking back at Paul or his dog. But as he was driving home, a thought from the day kept bothering him. *Why do I keep doing the things that I don't want to do, like rejecting Paul and other good things in my life?*

CHAPTER 6
THE STRUGGLE

"Wait, can you say that again?" Chad asked in disbelief. The crowded hallway was noisy enough to muffle the sound of his voice.

"Answer keys, Chad, answer keys! I've been working on this for a few years, but I've finally found a backdoor into each teacher's computer. And it's all in this little guy here." Aiden held up a small, thumb-sized USB drive. "All I gotta do is plug this thing into the back of a computer, and I get all the test answers for that class. The *entire class*, Chad! Get in quick, strike, and get out before they even know we were there. I call it, The Viper Protocol. Once I have them, I sell the answers to our fellow class-mates, and everyone wins!"

"Aiden, that's not—that's not legal!" Chad whisper-shouted.

"Hold up," Aiden said, a crooked smile on his face. "Don't get all preachy on me. Besides, you're the one who gave me your number so you could *get* these answers for our last statistics test."

Chad could feel his face flush with anger, and he poked his finger in Aiden's face. "What are you talking about? You just sent me that thing. I didn't look at it!"

Aiden crossed his arms and looked down his nose at Chad. "You'll have a tough time explaining that to Professor Simmons, won't you, Chad? Looks pretty bad to me."

Chad opened his mouth to shoot back, but Aiden put a hand on his shoulder. "Chad, you seem like a good guy, and I'm not trying to get you in trouble. I'm offering you quick, easy cash and perfect test scores for the rest of your time here. We both know the whole game here is rigged when 'College,'" Aiden put the word in air quotes, "is concerned. They bleed you dry, getting you into thousands of dollars of debt, then they pull the rug out from under you just when you think you're done!"

Chad thought back to the one missing credit, and all the extra work it had caused for him. Aiden continued, "This isn't a high-pressure sell. If you want in, you simply say the word, and I'll make sure you get set up. It's a short-term job with long-term benefits. Think of it as ... residual income. You and I split every sale we make. Wouldn't it be nice to treat yourself a little bit as you're finishing up school? Heck, you could even stop working at that disgusting laundry place."

Chad frowned, his mind racing. *Man, it would be nice to not eat microwave hot dogs every night, and earn some extra cash. But I don't know if I could live with myself if I went through with this.*

Aiden noticed the look on his face, and said sympathetically, "I'll give you some time to think about it."

As he turned and walked away, another more concerning thought entered Chad's mind. *Will I even be able to graduate if this all goes south?*

After another four nights of restless sleep, Chad had a hard time focusing on sorting the dirty mechanic uniforms in front of him. This week had been a strange one, as Chad found himself sometimes wishing to be on the trail with Paul, wanting the opportunity to ask some of his deeper questions, and at other times happy to retreat into his own head to think.

If what Paul's saying is true, why doesn't it line up with what I'm experiencing? It's obvious Paul hasn't had to struggle like I have. I don't think he gets it.

The week had been rather uneventful so far: no run-ins with Micah at work and he had been able to stay on top of his homework. As he was gathering his things to leave work on Friday, he spotted a piece of paper taped to the announcement corkboard.

It was a posting for a floor supervisor position, and one glance at the pay sent his thoughts racing. *Man, could I use this! I wouldn't have to sort filthy laundry all day, and I'd be paid more to do it! I'm the only one here who's almost a college grad. If anyone's going to be supervising, it should be me.*

Chad resolved to talk to Gary, the floor manager, about applying for the position. The hope of working less and earning more helped carry him through the rest of his week. If Chad was honest, he didn't see himself working at WeSort4U very long past graduation, but it was a means to an end.

When Saturday morning rolled around, Chad was excited to share his plan with Paul, but decided to wait for dramatic effect. As usual, Paul was waiting for him when he arrived, but didn't say anything until about a minute into their Bernard Peak hike, when Paul asked, "Good morning, Chad, how was your week?"

"It was fine, I guess. I've been thinking a lot about what you said last week, and I had something I couldn't figure out," Chad said.

"What's that?"

"Well, you said God wants us to work hard for him, right? My question is, why? Like, we supposedly work hard to please him, so when we die we don't have to go to hell? What purpose is there in work if it doesn't matter in the end?"

"Chad, that's a great question, and honestly not one often explored or focused on. Do you have your notebook handy?"

"Yeah, it's right here," Chad said, fishing it out of his back pocket.

"Good, let's begin. We are assured our reward, our prize, will be an inheritance, something passed down that is of incredible value. The word *inheritance* in Scripture is a term that excludes the notion of it being earned by works, but is fulfilled only by grace."

"What do you mean by inheritance?" Chad asked.

"Well, so many people believe, as I did for many years, inheritance is what we will receive up in heaven, after we pass on. The belief working from our whole being will pay off once we get past the pearly gates is only part of the story.

"Because God is love, our inheritance from him is also his grace and relationship with him now, here on earth as well as the gift of an abundant life. One definition of inheritance in Webster's 1828 Dictionary is that love is meant to be 'possessed and enjoyed in the here and now,'

"This means that following Colossians 3:22 not only secures future inheritance and blessings, but the real relationship found in drawing close to God in our everyday work while we are here on earth. We get to benefit from connection with him each day, no matter what the task is. This means what I do becomes very insignificant compared to why I do it and who I do it for."

"Let me get this straight," Chad said, a hand to his temple. "Work serves a much bigger purpose, and what I'm doing now has an eternal impact? This is kinda some heavy stuff to start off with."

"You're right, Chad, but we're getting into the true benefits of our work, and I don't mean pay or a great dental plan."

Chad rolled his eyes and sighed, enjoying the joke.

Chuckling, Paul said, "When you boil it all down, we work for an audience of one. God's given us life and an opportunity to serve him first, and when we do that with our whole heart, we get to bless those around us and realize the blessings of our connection with him."

"That's pretty cool, I guess," Chad said, nodding. "I've got some news though."

"You do?" Paul asked, turning his head and raising his eyebrows.

"I do! There's this promotion for floor supervisor where I work, and I'm going to interview for it on Monday. It's got, like, double the pay I have now and I wouldn't have to max out my credit card. I'd be able to pay for school and my living expenses, not to mention the benefits like ..."

Chad rambled on for several minutes, explaining how great the job was and how it could help him. Eventually, he stopped to take a breath and then asked, "So, what do you think?"

"I can see you've put a lot of thought into this, Chad. Are you sure you want my thoughts?"

"Of course!" Chad said, preparing for some sort of wisdom on how to nail the interview process.

"Don't do it."

Chad's smile slowly transformed into a confused frown. "I'm sorry?"

"Don't interview for the position. I don't think you're ready for it, and

I have so much more to teach you that would be invaluable for this course of action."

The ever-so-familiar vat of bubbling anger in Chad's chest began to rise up as his offense grew. "Why? You don't think I'm good enough? Have I not worked hard enough?"

"Chad, let me ask you a question: What do you think your starting place is when it comes to this position?"

Chad couldn't believe it. Was this old man really going to talk him out of something that was good for him? It was obvious to Chad: making more money and having less stress was what he needed, not waiting and walking instead through some stupid twelve-week program Paul had set up for him.

Chad laughed sarcastically. "You know what, I'm not gonna do this. I know what's going on here: you're jealous! You say you want me to grow and succeed, but obviously you don't! You're just a sad old man who can barely make it up and down a hill. What do you know about struggles in work and careers?"

Chad felt out of control, his chest heaving. He felt justified in his mind, but his heart told him he was making a huge mistake. He shut out that line of thinking as he continued with his tirade. "I'm done, Paul," he said, spitting out the name. "You know your way back down. I'll get this promotion on my own, like everything else in my life."

He wheeled around and stomped a few steps down the trail, then as an afterthought, added, "You don't even know what love is!"

He all but ran back to his car, tears forming in his eyes. His heart was crying out with despair at what he had done, even as his head felt justified by the outburst.

When Chad got back to his apartment, he kicked off his shoes and flopped down on his couch. He turned on the TV, trying to block out the thoughts filling his head. But as the sound droned on, the exhaustion of a week's worth of restless sleep caught up with him, and soon he was passed out on the couch, his turbulent dreams a reminder of what he had just done.

CHAPTER 7
WALKING THE TRAIL ONLY YOU CAN

C had awoke to the beep of his alarm from the other room. He stirred, the awful crick in his neck reminding him of his night spent on the couch. He ran a hand through his greasy hair and exhaled, coughing as he smelled his breath. Thoughts of his rant toward Paul started to fill his head as he pieced together the previous day's events.

He pulled out his phone, and couldn't believe what he found. It was eight a.m. on — *Sunday morning?! I've got a day and a half of homework to do, and I have to start my shift by three!*

Chad longed to sink back into the couch and ignore his responsibilities, but somehow, with a heavy heart and a sore body, he managed to get up and begin preparing for the day. As he worked, he subconsciously grappled with the guilty feelings and thoughts about his rant toward Paul, but eventually his mind won out and locked those feelings away, deep inside himself.

He knew how to do this well. He'd been doing it his whole life when thoughts of his father crept into his mind.

By two o'clock, he had made a sizable dent in his homework, so he decided to get ready for work, mentally shifting into thoughts about the impending interview on Monday.

As he worked his shift, he thought about all the reasons why the company should promote him and imagined how the conversation would go.

He decided he would focus on his ability to show up on time, that he was smarter than the average sorter, and the fact that he was completing his degree in business management. He found it ironic that he didn't understand how to manage his own life, or where he was going after school, but Chad was sure his ambition and drive would more than make up for his lack of experience with the company and job history overall.

Gary, Chad's manager, arranged for a thirty-minute interview on Monday before Chad started work at three. Chad showed up right on time, and was waved into Gary's office, where they sat down opposite each other.

Chad had decided to wear one of his nicer tee shirts, jeans, and a baseball cap. He made sure that he had showered and that his hygiene was on point, and since it was a step up from what he'd normally look like, he was sure it would earn him extra points.

He had brought in a copy of his resume for Gary to review, even though it was the same one he had provided months before. *If it was good enough then, he figured, it should be good enough now.*

As Chad sat across from Gary, he started feeling tension and nervousness rising up within him. *Why am I nervous? I work with Gary every day. I know I'm the best person for this job. Now I just need to act like it.*

Gary, his deep baritone voice reverberating around the small room, started off the interview by saying, "So, Chad, tell me why you decided to apply for this position."

"Well, Gary, I guess I figured I was one of the most qualified workers you have here at WeSort4U, and I believe in the work that we're doing here every day," Chad said, trying to sound convincing.

"Oh, well that's ... that's great, Chad," Gary said, a bit surprised. "Can you tell me what our company mission statement is and what it means to you?"

The blood started to drain from Chad's face as he realized that the first time, and last time, he had read the company's mission statement was his first day of orientation. His mind desperately scrambled as he tried to remember.

As he fumbled in his thoughts, Chad stammered, "You know, Gary, I really feel like, uh, what we do here and helping our customers have clean ... clean laundry that's sorted on time is, it's really important to me, and I want to keep that going. For our team, you know, in this new position."

Gary looked up from the notes he was taking and said, "I see," his flat and emotionless voice worrying Chad to no end. "Chad, tell me a bit about the team that you would be managing. Tell me about some of the strengths you see from your co-workers."

Chad's mind was racing a hundred miles a minute. He didn't know any of the sorters that well, besides Micah, for obvious reasons. He stayed to himself, and if he was being honest, saw his co-workers as more of an annoyance than anything else. He also realized that he wasn't quite sure who on his team he would be supervising, which seemed like a pretty big mistake at the moment.

"Well, I think we've got a pretty good crew overall. I'd say some I know better than others, but Micah is the team member I know the best."

At the mention of Micah, Gary peered up with a look of surprise and suspicion.

"Chad, since you mentioned Micah, help me understand how you would help manage and be a supervisor that supports him."

Chad did his very best to try to mask the disgust on his face when talking about Micah. "Gary, I'm not exactly sure how things will go with Micah, but I'm sure that when I have a position of authority over him, he'll be a lot more likely to fall in line and do what he's told."

Gary pursed his lips, made another note, then stood up. "I think I have a much better understanding now of your thoughts and potential fit for this position. I appreciate your time, and don't want to keep you from the start of your shift."

Gary reached out his hand, which Chad eagerly shook. *I must've done better than I thought!*

"No problem, sir." Chad replied, then turned and walked out the door, a spring in his step. *That promotion's as good as mine!*

≈

Chad's thoughts were filled all week with what his new position would hold, and what he'd spend his extra money on. On Friday, he sat sorting in eager expectation of the announcement that was sure to come.

I wonder if they'll order me some business cards. Maybe I can talk them into letting me use the spare office! I could put in a desk and a chair, stuff so I can relax when I need a break from being on the floor. Ooh! I could even–

His mental revelry was interrupted by a flick on his ear. "Ouch!" His hand reached up to clutch the side of his head. The snide voice of Micah entered his good ear, as unwelcome as ever.

"Ooh, sorry, didn't see you there," Micah said, walking to Chad's other side and flicking his right ear. Chad stood, fists clenched, teeth gritted in anger. He cocked his right arm back, fed up way past his limit, when he thought, *I can't punch one of my subordinates; that'd look bad.*

He lowered his hand, hating every second of Micah's sneer. He sat back down and tried to focus all his attention on the laundry bag in front of him.

"Good choice, Chaddy-baby," Micah said, coming around behind Chad's chair. He leaned in close and whispered, "It would look bad if you hit your new floor supervisor."

Chad shot to his feet, his chair crashing to the ground, and shoved Micah in the chest. "Shut up! Stop lying!"

Micah's sneer turned sadistic as he glared at Chad, then lifted up his new badge to reveal his name and new position. "I don't like your attitude, Chadwick," he said, his voice dripping with venom. Then he shouted loud enough for his entire crew to hear, "Everyone, stop what you're doing. Chad's going to sort the rest for us today!"

A cheer went up around the factory floor as fifteen people leaped out of their seats and headed toward the break room, leaving their piles of dirty laundry on the tables. Chad's stomach dropped as he realized he'd be working way past midnight.

Micah leaned in close once more. "Have fun, loser." With that, he sauntered away, leaving Chad with nothing but burning rage and two hundred pounds of clothes to sort.

~

At one thirty a.m, Chad staggered bleary-eyed into his apartment, empty. He knew that instead of his life getting easier—finding a way out of maxing out his credit card, no longer having to sort clothes, and gaining more time for homework and relaxation—his life was about to become a living hell at work.

Up until now he had fairly successfully blocked Paul out of his mind. But now with his mental barriers down, he didn't even know if he had the capacity to go and hike with him. The guilt and pain in his heart consumed him. All the self righteousness and justifications he had made in his mind crumbled as they were laid bare to one simple truth: *Paul was right.*

He flopped onto his bed, trying to allow the warm arms of sleep to pull him into their embrace, but there was something inside him that wouldn't let it happen. At two a.m., he decided it just wasn't going to work. He pulled himself out of bed, put on his tennis shoes and jacket, got in his car, and pulled out of the parking lot. The silver moon, surrounded by a sea of stars, shone light into his car, the ever-present glow comforting him a bit.

Without thinking about it, Chad silently drove to the Tubb's Hill trail-head where he had first met Paul and started this whole journey. He parked his car, then hiked up the trail. He remembered how Paul had questioned him about his purpose and what he was on the earth to do. Chad was about a quarter of the way up the mountain when he spotted a small clearing to the right of the trail, where the trees were sparse and allowed for a clear view of Lake Coeur d'Alene.

In the middle of the expanse Chad spotted two figures silhouetted against the moonlit sky, sitting on a bench. One was most definitely a person, while the other seemed to be an animal of some sort.

Chad tried to be quiet, thinking he'd find somewhere else to ponder things, and crept up the trail so as not to disturb them. As he was about to pass, he noticed the figure had a leg brace on one leg, and a cane resting on his knees. The animal was a dog with a leash attached to its collar.

No way. There's no way. "Paul?" Chad's single word whispered into the darkness.

"There's plenty of room on this bench, Chad. Why don't you sit down?"

Chad was convinced he was either dreaming or hallucinating, or maybe a combination of both, as he sat down beside Paul and Grace.

"How...why...why are you here? It's after two in the morning."

"Well, Chad, every Friday night I come out to this spot and spend time looking at the beautiful sunset, and I pray for all those who are important to me ... and that includes you. I'll typically get up and go back home after sunset, but for some reason I can't explain, I felt like God asked me to stay here. As you probably have guessed, I'm no night owl, so staying out here this late isn't a normal habit for me. But I think I now know why he asked me to stick around."

"Paul, I-I just ... I don't know, why do you treat me like this?" His stammered words were not accusatory or blaming, just pure wonder. "I've never been cared for like this from anyone, especially when ... I don't deserve it." Chad hung his head, ashamed of who he was. "I treated you like dirt. Why would you be out here praying for me, or even thinking about me?"

"For a couple of reasons, Chad. First off, it's because I know how much my own Father loves me, and cares for me, and does the exact same thing. I'm not talking specifically about my earthly father, who was a good man to be sure, but my heavenly Father, whose love for me never changes. It's unconditional, eternal, and built on his character, not my own. Also, Chad, if I'm being honest, I think my son would've been a lot like you."

Chad's head lifted at this comment. "You ... you have a son?"

"Yes, I had a son and a beautiful wife ... who left this earth much too soon. Or at least, much sooner than I would've liked. Seventeen years ago, on this very night, my wife, son and I were headed out of town for a quick weekend trip, when a car in the other lane veered into us and hit us head on. My son was six at the time, and ..." Paul paused, a tear glistening on his cheek, "I was the only one to survive."

Chad was silent as Paul continued. "You see, back then I wasn't the man I am today. I was arrogant and full of pride. I didn't treat them like I should have, or cherish them for who they were created to be. My son

Charlie would've been your age if he was still down here with us. And so ... I only want the best for you."

At this, a sob built in Chad's throat, and twin tears made their way down his cheeks. He began to cry, quietly at first and then, rocking back and forth, he finally released all the emotions he had worked so hard to shield from everyone, including himself.

"Paul, I-I ... I am so sorry. I'm so sorry for how I treated you last week, and how I've treated you since we met. I've questioned your intentions, your motivations, and your ... your love and care for me. I just feel lost, and-and hopeless and so scared. I want so badly to do the right things ... I just don't think I can do this." Chad paused, taking a deep shuddering breath before continuing, "I can't continue living this life."

"Chad, your desperation, your cry for help, and your willingness to live differently, is all the Father needs to radically change every area of your life. The love you felt from me is just a small-scale picture of God's love for you."

As tears streamed down from Chad's eyes, he let out a loud cry. "But how do I make it real? How do I do it? I've seen it in your life. I can see it, I can feel that there's something ... even my mom can see ...." With desperation in his voice, Chad asked Paul, "How do I make him real to me?"

With a calm, loving voice, Paul said, "The Bible states that Jesus stands and knocks at the threshold of our hearts, and that anyone who opens the door to receive him, will have him in their heart forever. Chad, the first step is to let him in. Let him into every single part of your life."

Paul's voice rose with intensity as he declared, "He wants to give you the power and love for every area, every situation. He wants to be a part of your schooling, to help you finish strong and with integrity. He wants to give you strength as you are working and figuring out how to love your co-workers ...." The corner of Paul's mouth turned up in a small smile. "Even Micah. He wants to direct your career and promote you, at the right time, and in the right way. Chad ... are you ready to give your whole heart to Jesus, and allow him to guide your life?"

With a resolve and determination that Paul had never seen before, and with heaven's light shining within his eyes, Chad said, "I am. I ... I know now that I need to live my life differently. And you've been right, Paul, about ... well, about everything. I truly am sorry."

Paul's eyes filled once again with tears of gratitude and excitement. "Chad, my boy, you've just stepped onto the right path. Seeing where we've been wrong, asking for help, and making things right, are the first steps into your heavenly Father's loving arms."

Chad cracked a small smile, and it soon enveloped his entire face. It was evident, even by the sparse amount of natural light, that he felt an immense sense of relief, as if a massive burden had been lifted off his soul.

They spent a few moments in silence, then Chad looked at his phone, the bright light almost blinding him. "Oh my gosh, Paul. It's four a.m. We're supposed to hike tomorrow."

They chuckled together, until Paul said, "Well, technically, Chad, it is tomorrow. What if we stayed here a little longer, and kept talking."

CHAPTER 8
PREPARE FOR THE JOURNEY

The warm summer sunrise greeted Chad, Paul, and Grace as it rose over the hills to start the day. They had decided during the course of their conversation to hike together on the rather difficult trail. Chad had opened up more than he ever had in his life during the wee hours of the morning, telling Paul about his father, his childhood and where he came from, and where he hoped to go.

"So, Chad, in what ways do you think your father's choice, leaving you and your mother when you were young, has impacted who you are today and where you see yourself going?"

"I think I've let it define me in more ways than I realized, up to this point," Chad said. "I can see how my anger started with my dad leaving, but it spilled over into every other area of my life. It ... it's ended up robbing me of my joy and purpose in my school, work, and relationships."

"I'm sorry, Chad ... a father is supposed to be someone who takes you under his wing and helps you navigate life. He should've been that for you," Paul said, placing his hand on Chad's shoulder. He continued, "We all have the capacity to fail in our relationships, but it's impossible for your heavenly Father to fail you."

"That's so hard to wrap my mind around," Chad said. "I mean, I've been doing things on my own for so long, it's hard to imagine trusting somebody else to help me."

"That's understandable. It'll take some relearning to be a child with a father who loves you and will never leave you."

"A child?" Chad asked, confusion evident in his voice.

"Yes. God asks us to become like a child in our faith, believing he will do what he says he will do," Paul explained.

"Oh! I get it. Like when I was learning to swim, and my mom would tell me to jump into the pool and she'd catch me. I believed her, and so I did it!"

"Why did you believe her?" Paul asked.

"Well ... I guess because of the thousands of other times she'd proven herself to me. She'd never given me a reason to doubt her, so my trust in her was bigger than my fear," Chad said.

"That's a good connection you're making, Chad," Paul said, nodding. "In the same way, we can choose to trust God in spite of the fear we have. He's more than proven himself, by sending his Son to die for us."

They were quiet for a moment, as Chad pondered his statement, but they hadn't gone far when Paul said, "Chad, do you still have that notebook with you, by chance? I think we'll talk about some things you'll probably want to write down."

Chad put a hand to his forehead, "Sheesh, Paul, I feel like I could fill twenty notebooks with everything we've been talking about."

Paul smiled knowingly. "I know, and I'm so grateful for that. I want to talk with you a bit about preparing for this new path that you've decided to go on. That actually brings us to our fifth principle: **Prepare for the Journey**."

"What do you mean by that? How do I prepare, if you said I'm already on the path?" Chad asked with a sincere tone in his voice.

Paul stopped on the trail for a moment and said, "Let me pull something from Grace's pack here."

Chad had never paid attention to it before, but he soon realized what he had assumed to be a dog-vest, meant to keep Grace warm, carried the items Paul began listing.

"Let's see here, I've got some water," he said as he began placing the objects on the ground next to him, "some beef jerky, a first aid kit, three emergency blankets—"

"Three?"

"Yes, one for you, one for me, and one for Grace. Then a fire-starting kit, and that's all."

Chad was impressed so much thought had gone into something as simple as hiking gear. "Why would you bring all this on our hikes?"

"Chad, ever since my 'I'm on the road' adventure from my college days, I've tried to be as prepared as possible for the journey ahead. No one can plan to be prepared for everything, but I do believe we can have the right tools, just in case. The same should apply to our life, our work, and our walk with Jesus," Paul said as he began to put everything back in the vest.

"What tools can I use to be prepared for work and life?" Chad asked, pulling the small notebook out of his pocket.

Paul regained his feet, and they started forward. "Well, one of them is tackling the toughest things first. You see, Chad, many times people tend to leave the harder things for last, either because they're overwhelmed or choose to put it off. By doing the toughest things first every day, you'll find that your time is more enjoyable and you can give attention to other endeavors."

"That makes sense. I normally put off my statistics homework, or the stinkiest pile of laundry to sort, until last. And I dread it all day, too."

"Yes, this principle is good when it comes to having difficult conversations and dealing with situations, giving them the attention they deserve."

"Okay," Chad said, scribbling with his pencil. "Got that one down. What's the next tool?"

"The next one is praying out loud for wisdom in every area of your life. One of my favorite authors, Marilyn Howshall says 'Love carries wisdom with it, and wisdom always carries love. The two are connected, you can't have one without the other.' In light of this, when we pray and ask our loving heavenly Father for wisdom, out loud, we're activating our faith and making it real."

"That's interesting," Chad said, rubbing his chin.

Paul paused, reaching into his pocket. He pulled out a palm-sized silver compass. "To me, it's like this compass. It only works because I know and believe that there is a true North. I don't question if the compass will change its mind at some point or if it has bad intentions toward me. It faithfully guides me along my journeys because I know what it is capable of doing and I have learned to use it. Prayer, which is truly having conversations with your loving Father, is the same way."

"I've never heard people pray out loud before," Chad said, "except maybe in movies when they say grace." At the mention of her name, Grace perked up and gave Chad her full attention. The two men laughed.

Paul nodded. "When we're no longer confining the Creator of our universe in our head, we make him real and bring him into the intimate parts of our lives. Prayer is simply a conversation. It doesn't have to be anything showy, just a heartfelt chat between you and the Lord. Just like the chats we've been having together."

"Wow, that's good, Paul. Okay, I got that one. What else?"

"Chad, have you ever been crabbing before?"

"Ummm ... no, I've been to the Oregon coast a few times, but I've never gone crabbing. Why?" Chad asked.

"Well, you see, when you catch live crabs and put them in a bucket, an interesting thing happens. While any one crab can easily escape, its efforts will be undermined by the others, ensuring their collective demise." Paul said, pushing a sharp rock off the path with his cane.

"What do you mean?"

"Well, if one crab tries to climb out, the others will pull it back down so they themselves can get out. If one crab tries too hard or often enough, the others will break its leg to keep it from going on."

"Why would they do that?" Chad asked, aghast. "If they keep hurting each other they're all cooked ... literally."

"That's the point, Chad. Instead of learning from and helping each other, the goal is to keep each other oppressed and with an attitude of, 'If I can't have it, neither can you.' The workplace and life are much the same. Instead of people learning from each other's mistakes, or helping each other and bringing out the best, they're focused on pulling others down. They live in a place of resentment, jealousy, and competition. Have you had any feelings like this toward anyone lately?" Paul asked, gazing at him with a caring look in his eyes.

Chad hung his head. "Yeah," he said sadly. "Micah. Since his promotion...that's going to be rough."

"You're right, Chad. How you treat Micah, and honestly the fruit of all your relationships, will be the ultimate test and guidepost to help you ensure you're staying on the right path."

"I'm ... I'm not sure I follow what you're trying to say with this one," Chad said, straining to understand.

"Another thing Marilyn talks about is that the fruit of our relationships is the truest reflection of who we are and shows us the path we're on. I imagine it's fairly easy to get along with people who treat you well; everyone can do that. It's also easier to treat others better than you do your family. You can oftentimes take those that you're closest to for granted because you assume you'll always have them." Chad realized with a start that he had received a message from his mother asking him to call her back, and it'd been over a week. He then thought of Mrs. B, his advisor, and how much she'd done to try and help Chad out, and how Chad had treated her.

"So ... you're saying who I am is defined by who I love and how I treat others, those closest to me, my family, and even people like Micah?"

"Yes, Chad. Because Jesus loves us through his relationship with us, it's his standard of love that helps us see if we're on the right course, or if we've veered off. Status, personal achievement, accumulating wealth, or anything else this world deems valuable, is worthless by comparison."

"I'm glad I was able to make things right with you, Paul," Chad said, "but I think I need to do the same with ... pretty much everyone!"

"By making things right with those you need to, you now get to start from a new place in how you treat them and how you love them. As a reminder, not everyone may receive your changed heart right away, or even in the way you would like, but it's not about them and their response, it's about you and the Lord."

Chad sighed. "I think I get it now, Paul ... but this isn't going to be easy."

He began writing down the names of people he had wronged. He was still writing a few minutes later when they reached the trailhead, marking the end of their hike.

"Now that you know the next steps to take," Paul said as they walked to the parking lot, "and you've been prepared with the tools to get where you need to go, it's up to you to partner with what God wants for you, and launch yourself down the path he's laid out for you."

"Thank you so much, Paul. Your encouragement means so much to me. Is there any way we could grab coffee together sometime this week?"

"You bet," Paul said, a gleam in his eye. "Would Tuesday morning work?"

"Sure!" Chad took a deep breath. "All right, I'm ready."

CHAPTER 9
LIVING IN YOUR STRENGTHS

When Chad entered the coffee shop that Tuesday morning, Paul was already sitting at a table, waiting for him. As he walked to the table, Chad couldn't help but admire the interior: a mix of dark woods, industrial piping, modern light fixtures, and unpainted brick that managed to be inspiring and cozy at the same time. Paul's table was situated in front of a roaring fireplace, and it popped and crackled as Chad sat down.

"Good morning, Chad," Paul said. "You're looking a bit more chipper today."

Chad smiled broadly, his grin stretching from ear to ear. "I do feel a lot better, Paul. I know it sounds weird, but I feel almost ... lighter."

"So what new fad diet have you been trying?" Paul asked with a wink.

Chad let out a laugh louder than he intended, which attracted the attention of several people ordering their drinks. He covered his mouth with his hand, embarrassed, and then it was Paul's turn to laugh.

"Being honest," Chad said, "I've never apologized to so many people in my life."

"Chad, you've done more than apologize. You have true, heartfelt repentance for the wrongs you've done and the people you've hurt. By making things right with the people closest to you and with God, you now get to experience the freedom that decision provides."

Chad rubbed his cheek. "Yeah, I gotta admit, the hardest person to talk to by far was Micah. I ... what's the word ... repented to my mom and to Mrs. B, and they totally accepted it and were happy for me, but it was a different story last night."

～

"Micah!" Chad called out, jogging across the parking lot toward his new boss, who was just getting into his car.

Once Chad reached the vehicle, Micah asked flatly, "What do you want, Chad?"

"Micah, I ... I just—"

"Spit it out, Chad, I'm trying to go home," Micah said. "It's not easy dealing with all the pressures of being a floor supervisor, but you wouldn't know anything about that, would you?"

In the darkness, Chad felt his old anger trying to come back up to the surface, but only for a brief moment. Under his breath, he murmured, "Help me, God. Give me strength."

"What was that?"

He decided to blurt it all out at once. "Micah, I'm sorry for how I've treated you. I've threatened to hurt you, insulted you, and I know you've experienced a lot of pushback and resistance from me. I promise you, I'll give my very best here at work, and that you won't have to experience any of those things anymore from me."

Micah looked taken aback, and he was speechless for a moment before he shook his head and sneered. "Whatever,"

With that, Micah got in his car and slammed the door, wheeling out of the parking lot. Chad let out a combination sigh and "Thank you" in the quiet darkness.

～

"Chad, I'm proud of you," Paul said once Chad had finished his story. "That took a lot of courage. I know you need that job, especially over the next few weeks, to help you stay afloat until you graduate. I think God will continue to use your workplace in powerful and unexpected ways. Now your heart is pointed in the right direction, we can focus on the practical steps to fill your career and life with purpose. When your head and your heart are right with God, and your relationships are right with those around you, God can take you places in your life and career you never could've gone on your own."

Chad reached into the backpack he'd brought with him, pulled out a full-size notebook and pencil, and began to write in it. Paul raised an eyebrow. "Going rather heavy-duty, aren't we?"

"I don't want to miss a single piece of what we're going to talk about," Chad said playfully, "thus, big notebook." He grinned and wiggled his eyebrows.

"Perfect. I want to talk about our sixth principle: **Living in Your Strengths**. We are going to spend some time talking about your strengths, and how by discovering and nurturing the things you're good at, you can help keep yourself on the right path. Imagine if you and I decided to go next week and hike Everest together."

"I don't think I'd make it," Chad said, looking up from his notebook.

"Neither would I," Paul said, "because we haven't built up the endurance. You see, we have to have an accurate picture of where we are, and how we can improve, in every area of life, because only through aggressive challenges can we assess and grow in our strengths. That's why we have progressed to more challenging hikes as our weeks together have gone on."

"Makes sense," Chad said, cocking his head, "but how do I find out what my strengths are? Where did they come from?"

"You see, we are all fearfully and wonderfully made, knitted together in the womb by God's master hand. He's given you specific and unique skills and talents he's put inside of you to serve him and others. Let me give you some practical ways to help you dig a bit deeper, to discover what God's put in you to do."

Chad wrote down a few more notes, then turned to a new page. "Okay, shoot."

"One of the best ways to know what some of your natural strengths are is to ask your friends and family, those who are closest to you. Sometimes the things we're good at are the things we tend to overlook. For instance, as I've gotten to know you a bit better, one of the strengths I've seen in you is your perseverance, your ability to move forward when things get tough."

Chad put his pencil down. "I don't feel that way at all. I mean, I've been working hard at my job and school, but I literally just hit a breaking point a few days ago."

"I get that, Chad. I also see how you've been able to continue moving forward when you've had some pretty big hurdles in your life. I bet if you spoke with your mom this week and asked her this question, she'd be able to give you more insight into some of the natural strengths you've displayed from your childhood up until today," Paul said, leaning back in his seat and placing his hands behind his head.

They were quiet for a moment, the only sound between them the scraping of Chad's pencil. Then he said, "Okay, I can do that. What's next?"

"Since we're talking about childhood, I want you to think back to your six-year-old self."

Chad flinched. "You know, that wasn't a great time in my life. I don't remember too much about it."

Leaning forward and putting his elbows on the table, Paul said. "I understand, Chad. I'm sure that was hard for you and your mother. But I want you to look back on the good things, the things that you enjoyed doing at that age. For many of us, between the ages of six and eight is the time when we have the purest expression of who we are and what's within us.

"An example from back when I was a child, and I didn't realize this until later, is I loved to lead. I would pretend I was blazing a trail through the wilderness for my parents and brothers when we went on hikes together. As I grew older, I came to recognize I had somewhat unintentionally found opportunities to serve and help others through leadership. This led to the formation of my own small company many years later."

"That's something I've been meaning to ask," Chad said. "What exactly did you do before you retired?"

"I promise I'll get to that, but I want to keep walking through these next few steps about your strengths. Does that sound good to you?" Paul asked.

"Yeah, of course."

"Another great way," Paul said, "is to take the 'Strengths Finder Assessment' online. It's a small investment of your time and money, but the results will help you see where you're strongest, and maybe where you're not as strong."

"Oh, cool, so then I'll know where my weaknesses are, so I can work on them and be more well-rounded?" Chad asked, nodding his head in agreement with himself.

"Actually, Chad, the point of discovering and focusing on our strengths in these specific ways is to grow and enhance them. You'll naturally feel like your authentic true self when you're working and completing tasks that honor your strengths," Paul said, shifting his weight on his chair. He continued, "For me, my strengths point to my ability to connect and communicate well with others. I love leading through service and connecting however I can. I'm a people person.

"One of my weaknesses is analyzing reports and working through spreadsheets. It's a task I don't enjoy, and don't have a passion for. You see, Chad, I can spend my time trying to get incrementally better," Paul said, raising two fingers and pointing to the space between them, "at something I don't enjoy and am not naturally gifted at, or I can pour my time, attention, and focus into developing the strengths God put in me. Those are areas I can grow exponentially in."

"I think I understand," Chad said, "but it kinda seems backwards from what I've heard so often throughout my life."

"I agree, that is what the world often tells us. Let me give you another example. Let's pretend for a moment you have a baseball and I ask you to go outside to the street corner, and throw the ball at the stop sign one block away. Which arm would you pick to throw the ball?"

"Well, I'm right handed, so I guess I'd choose my right?"

"And why is that?" Paul asked as he steepled his hands.

"It's the one I've used my whole life, the one I'm most comfortable with, and probably the one that's stronger and I would have the best chance of hitting the target," Chad said, trying his best to figure out what Paul was trying to say.

"Now, if I gave you ten throws with your right arm, how many of those throws do you think would hit the sign or get close?"

Chad chuckled. "Well, I was never great at baseball, so I don't know about hitting it, but I think I could get close six or seven times."

Paul let out a small laugh. "I bet you'd do great. Now, let's say you did the same exercise, but throwing with your left arm. How many times do you think you would get close?"

Chad breathed out and ran a hand through his hair. "Oh man, like ... maybe one and a half?"

"How would it feel to throw with your left arm that many times?"

"It'd feel awkward. I can't remember the last time I threw something with my left arm, and I can't imagine how tired it would be after ten throws!"

"You're absolutely right. Now let's say I gave you two weeks to prac- tice throwing, just with your left arm, one hundred throws per day. Do you think you'd do any better?" Paul asked, taking a sip of coffee.

"I don't know ... I think maybe I'd get it close, like, three times out of ten? But it'd take a while. I don't know if I'd ever feel as comfortable throwing with my left arm as I would with my right."

"Yeah, I bet you'd hit a few less parked cars if you practiced that much," Paul said, cracking a smile. "Now what if you did the two-week assignment using only your right arm? The same rules apply, how many times do you think you could get close to the sign?"

"Honestly? Nine out of ten times I could get close. I might be able to hit the sign once or twice," Chad said, mentally picturing the feat.

"I bet you could. You see, when we focus on our strengths, and take steps to increase them and make them stronger, we're focusing on what God gave us, fostering it and nurturing it, making it grow, instead of focusing on what he didn't give us. And so with my spreadsheets example from earlier, I don't want you to get the wrong impression: I still do that task to the best of my ability. It's just not an area of strength, nor does it fill my cup to do that activity. After I discovered this in work, I partnered with people who naturally love data analytics and spread- sheets, who could spend days upon days making comparisons and looking for trends. In turn, I'm able to help those same individuals with the people side of their work, so we're able to bring out the best in each other. Doesn't it seem better to work and get a lot better at what you're good at, than to get a little better at things you're not?"

"Wow, Paul," Chad said, shaking his head. "That's good. But now I gotta know: what did you do for work?"

"Well, after the whole insurance agent fiasco, I became a barista at a popular coffee chain, and rose to the position of manager. It was then that ..." —Paul trailed off for a moment, a faraway look in his eyes—"... the accident happened. After that, I had a real understanding of my own mortality and caught a vision for what I wanted to do with my life. While I loved managing the coffee shop, I wanted to connect people with the outdoors and the beauty of nature.

"I decided to ask God where he wanted me to start, and to help me focus on a need. One thing that was always hard for me when camping was finding a tent big enough for someone my size that was also well insulated. No matter how hard I tried I could never find anything that didn't end up falling apart after one season of use.

"And so I took to making tents in my garage. I learned how to build prototypes. My first few were pretty bad, but I continued to play around with different insulating materials. Ultimately, I called in a few friends who had the same love for the outdoors, and financial resources, to help me move my prototype from an idea to a reality.

"I continued to make tents, and my friends helped me find people to sell them to. I did everything I could think of—I went around to trade shows in my area, on weekends, to help promote the product, using my strength for speaking with people, to help sell the tents. I used the internet as well in the early days, when e-commerce was just taking off.

"Eventually, I was making enough money to quit my management position and make the tents full time. Soon, the demand was too great for me to handle alone, so I started hiring a few people at first, to help me create the tents. After only three years, my operation had grown to provide over three hundred jobs, and I brought on my initial investors to help me run the company day-to-day.

"Soon, we started branching out into other areas of outdoor equipment, focusing on quality and backing everything we sold with our one hundred percent money-back guarantee, as well as a lifetime warranty. If people were going to spend their hard-earned money for high-end equipment, we wanted them to know we were going to stand behind it, and have integrity with everything we did.

"Around that time, some commercial stores reached out to us, wanting to carry our product. It was slow at first. A few sales here, a few sales there. But, over time, our brand grew to nationwide, and now international, recognition. Today we have our own retail outlets so we can sell directly to our customers.

"We're currently the nation's largest, privately-owned outdoor supply company, providing thousands of jobs."

Chad sat back in his chair. "Hold on a second. What's your middle name?"

"James. Why?"

Chad's jaw would've hit the floor if it hadn't been attached to his head. "Are you telling me you're the founder of P.J. Outfitters?"

"Guilty as charged," Paul said, raising his hands.

"You've got to be kidding me!" Chad's voice rang with awe, tinged with disbelief. "I-I ... I don't even like camping and I know your brand!"

At this, a few of the other coffee shop patrons looked over at him, annoyance written all over their faces.

"Why didn't you tell me this earlier?" Chad asked.

"Chad, what I've learned and what I hope to continue to teach you, is that my value, my worth, and who I am, isn't tied up in any of what I just told you. If our company closed its doors tomorrow, it wouldn't change how God sees me, and that's all that really matters," Paul said earnestly. "It hasn't always been that way, though. The struggle to find out who you really are, and the principles I'm sharing with you, will not come without a price."

"What does that mean?" Chad asked, leaning forward.

"It means you're paying for coffee this morning."

This time, Chad didn't care how many dirty looks he got as the small coffee shop echoed with his laughter.

"But seriously, Chad, what I get to pass on to you comes from over thirty years of experience. You get to learn from my successes and mistakes as we keep learning and growing together. I want you to know how important this way of life is to me, but also how special it is that I get to share it with you."

"I feel the same way, Paul," Chad said, his voice cracking a bit.

They talked for a few more minutes, then Chad excused himself to use the restroom. When he got back to their table, he found nothing but a note in the place where Paul had been:

Chad, I lost track of time while we were talking, and realized I had another appointment I have to run to. Please use this gift to help with the strengthsfinder test. -Paul

Folded underneath the note was a crisp fifty dollar bill. With a lump in his throat, Chad collected his things and left the coffee shop, anticipating their next conversation.

CHAPTER 10
YOUR PERSONAL BEST

"And the bag of miscellaneous rags once again goes to ..." Micah dragged out the word in a game-show-host voice, drumming his fingers on the sorting table for added effect, "Chad! Congratulations. Please come take your prize!"

Chad rose out of his chair and walked toward Micah. Typically, the biggest bag, the bag of miscellaneous rags, had always been passed around every week, but not since Micah had gained power. Now it was almost Chad's exclusive property, on top of the mandatory load he had to do.

Micah lifted up the sack as Chad approached and placed it in his outstretched arms. "There you go! Now, Chad, what are you going to do with your fabulous winnings?" His voice dripped with sarcasm.

"Micah, I'm just grateful for the opportunity to have a job to come to every day," Chad said, portraying love and sincerity through his eyes.

There were a few audible gasps around the room, as the whole floor was now watching the exchange. No one, not even Micah, had expected Chad to say anything like that, considering their history. Micah fumbled with his words for a moment, and when he couldn't find any, Chad turned around and walked to his station, Micah sputtering behind him.

"Chad ... you ... uh ... well, I'm glad you like working, because you'll have plenty to do! Hope you're looking forward to that!" Micah's face transformed from one of speechless confusion to a snarl of loathing.

Micah had stormed off and Chad had started folding when a coworker, Thomas, came over. Chad hadn't made many friends in the factory before he had given his life to Jesus, but now with all the extra attention put on him by Micah, he was soon known to almost everyone in the plant.

"What are you doing?" Thomas asked, leaning on the table, eyes trained on the door in case Micah came back.

"Well, Tom, I'm learning that I don't work for Micah, or even WeSort4U. I work for God. He's my boss now, and I don't have to worry about pleasing anyone but him."

Thomas looked at Chad with wide eyes, scratched his head, then turned and walked back to his station, clearly contemplating what Chad had said.

The putter of Paul's electric bike engine contrasted with the quiet beauty of the Hiawatha Trail, adding a buzz to the otherwise silent forest. Paul had surprised Chad by taking him an hour away from Coeur d'Alene to ride on the famous bike path, and the instant they arrived, they'd been awed by the sheer scope and beauty of the area. Grace wasn't allowed on the trail, so it was just the two of them this time. Paul enjoyed the mostly downhill 15-mile ride, which was challenging but doable for his knee.

Chad enjoyed the car ride they had together to get to the trailhead, and had recounted the week's events, including what had been happening with Micah.

"So I've got to find something else ... anything else," Chad said now as he maneuvered his bike along the trail. "I can still work for God and not have to endure this punishment."

"I'm really proud of you for how you're responding to what's happening at work and with Micah in particular. I don't know if you're noticing it, but it seems like you're having a positive impact on those around you on the floor."

Chad tilted his head, pondering what Paul had said.

"I certainly think it makes sense to look for other opportunities and growth," Paul said, accelerating slightly to crest a small rise, "but I would be careful about having your main motivation be trying to escape the current spot you're in.

"I've seen this happen so many times, Chad, where people are so focused on escaping, that they don't spend the time solidifying who they are and where they're going. This can lead to trading one bad situation for another."

"Okay," Chad said, nodding as he twisted his handlebars to make a turn. "What would you suggest I do?" His tone of voice suggested he honestly wanted to know what Paul had to say.

Paul smiled and said, "This brings us to our seventh principle: **Your Personal Best**. Chad, what's your company's mission statement?"

"'To bring our customers the very best service we can provide, and exceed their expectations in every interaction,'" Chad said, quoting what he had memorized from the company website.

"Great! What's your personal mission statement?"

"Uh ... is this like 'who I am' type of thing again?"

"Not exactly. For example, my mission statement is 'to motivate and encourage others to see who they are in Christ, and to operate in his love, especially in the workplace.' This means my actions and motivations should reflect this, or I'm working outside God's intentions and plan for my life. I believe having a personal mission statement for our lives, and to help us frame our work life, is what's missing for so many. It can help direct our steps when we're not quite sure what's next or which direction to go."

Chad pulled over to the side of the trail and pulled his notebook out, quickly writing in it with frantic scratches, trying to record what Paul was saying. Paul pulled up beside him.

"So, should my strengths tie into this personal mission statement as well?" Chad asked.

Paul smiled broadly. "Did you complete your assessment already? What did it say?"

"Well, I enjoyed it, and it told me a lot about myself that I hadn't thought about much before. It said that 'achiever' was one of my top five strengths, and the definition said 'I like to work hard and possess a great deal of stamina and I'd take great satisfaction in being busy and productive.'"

Paul's smile widened. "That doesn't surprise me one bit. See, your mission statement can tie in with your achiever strength, and how you are relentless in your service to others."

Chad nodded his head in agreement, jotting a few more notes before he and Paul started again down the trail.

"You see, Chad, once you know who you are and where your strengths lie, you can start seeing a path for your career that previously seemed inaccessible, like we saw when we were at Mineral Ridge."

Chad thought back to the secret lookout that only Paul knew and smiled at the memory.

"I can see how a personal mission statement would be important to help guide me forward in my work, but how will it help me get a new, or better, job?"

"Well, this next step, along with the other steps we'll be talking about in the next few weeks, will help you find the right path for you," Paul said.

At that moment, Paul and Chad were riding over one of the many wood-trestle bridges along the Hiawatha route, the sound of trickling water below them seeming so far away. Paul slowed to a stop on his bike, gazing at the nature below and around them.

"I look at it this way: these trestle bridges make it possible to ride our bikes down this beautiful trail. Each bridge represents a connection point, and Chad, you've had so many connection points for your career and life just over the past few weeks," Paul said, closing his eyes and lifting his face toward the sun.

Chad nodded his head. "Yeah, that's definitely true."

"God is the great connector," Paul continued. "He creates bridges of understanding and wisdom to help us continue down the personal trail that only we can walk with him."

Paul remounted his bike, and he and Chad spent the rest of the morning riding down the Hiawatha, enjoying the scenery and views the trail provided. Once they reached the end, Paul said, "Chad, I know you've taken some good notes today. Why don't you work on what your personal mission statement is, so we can help to set you up for success with your future opportunities?"

"That sounds like a great plan," Chad said, grinning. "Thank you for taking me out here, Paul."

They loaded their bikes onto the shuttle bus that was waiting for them, rode back to the top of the trail, got into Paul's truck, and returned to town. Chad was ready for a new phase of life to begin.

CHAPTER 11
APPLY LIKE A SPY

"Chad, honey, you sound ... different. In a really good way!"

Chad was talking to his mom, catching her up on his week. "One part that's strange is that my circumstances are more stressful than ever. Schoolwork is still hard, and it's been more difficult for me to focus on finishing. Work is harder than ever with Micah's daily antics. And financially..." Chad's voice trailed off.

I can't say anything about that, he thought. I can't put that burden on her. Even though my credit card is going to be maxed out in the next few weeks. For a moment, seeing his need to graduate with a positive account balance, he felt a strong temptation to take Aiden up on his offer.

"...things are tight. But despite all that, I feel a sense of peace, Mom ...something I've never felt before."

Chad's mom had silent tears of gratitude rolling down her cheeks.

"I can't wait for you to meet Paul too, Mom."

"And to give you a heads up, I'm going to spoil you rotten when I get there," she said, her smile evident in the tone of her voice. "We're gonna get sushi, we're going to the beach, and I'm taking you to get one of those giant bowls of ice cream and cookies I keep hearing about! Who knows, maybe we'll even go on a hike!"

Chad groaned mockingly. "You want me to look forward to your visit, don't you, Mom?"

They laughed together for a moment. "No, really, Mom, I'm so excited to see you again. I love you so much."

"I love you too, Chad. Have a great time on your hike!"

Chad turned off his phone and went back to working on his mission statement. It had taken him longer than he anticipated, almost a week and a half, but he was extremely satisfied with the results.

It had been a good week for Chad. The Saturday hike with Paul had been an eye-opening conversation about work and life that he thoroughly enjoyed. During that week of working, as well, he'd noticed a shift in the dynamic of the plant.

At first, a few of his co-workers were curious as to why he was acting the way he was with Micah. Chad shared a few pieces of wisdom he had learned from Paul, trying to embody what God had done through him, and the men had an immediate response. They recognized the good ideas and inspiration Chad seemed to carry with him, and wanted more of it for themselves.

The sorters asking for his advice grew in number until, by the end of the week, he was more of a floor manager than Micah was, lovingly inspiring his shift crew to be the best they could. Ironically, Micah was the biggest thorn in his side.

Micah too sensed the power shift and didn't like it one bit. He had become unbearable, giving everyone extra work, forcing people to be punished by cleaning long after hours for breaking his ever-changing rules, or often for no reason at all.

The sorters collectively harbored a deep resentment toward Micah, but Chad combated it at every turn, telling the crew, "If you let Micah bring out the worst in you, you're giving in. Anyone can get angry and treat him wrong, but it takes a strong man to love him through it. Let Micah bring out the best in you. If you perform well under this kind of pressure, imagine what you'll be able to do without it!"

With all this happening around him, Chad was thirsty for the wisdom Paul could give him. They'd set up a hike that Saturday at Big Tree Trail, and before Chad knew it, he was beside his mentor passing the trailhead, beginning the hike with Grace following close behind. He realized in that moment that he actually enjoyed hiking with Paul. He enjoyed pushing himself further and further each time, pushing past his physical barriers.

"It sounds like you've had quite an eventful week, Chad," Paul said, a grin on his weathered face.

Chad sighed. "The majority of it has been spent on my personal mission statement, and although it's been a bit challenging, I'm proud of the end result."

"Would you care to share it with me?" Paul asked, an eager glint in his eyes.

Chad nodded. "It's, 'to serve others in the work that I do, and to lead by example as I learn how to love with the same love I've been given.'"

"That's amazing, Chad. I can tell you've put a lot of thought and time into expressing your 'why,'" Paul said with a wide smile.

"I have. Paul, do you think I'm ready to look for something new?"

"Chad, you're ready. Your head and heart are more aligned than ever, and while you're still learning to grow into who you're created to be, it doesn't feel like you're trying to run away from your current situation, like a few weeks back."

"Yeah, I think I'll probably be a little sad to leave the guys on the floor, if I get another opportunity elsewhere," Chad said, looking at the ground for a moment.

"Not if, Chad, when. When opportunities present themselves. Good opportunities have a way of finding good people. What we're going to go through today will help you, and bring in the elements of what we've learned so far to help you see the next step on your path."

"All right, sounds great! How do we start?" Chad said, springing over a small rock with excitement.

"Have you seen any good spy movies lately?" Paul asked, tilting his head.

"I'm sorry?"

Paul chuckled. "I know it's an odd question, but it'll undoubtedly help us in what we'll talk about today. You see, our eighth principle is: **Apply Like a Spy.**"

"Yeah, I've seen a few, I guess," Chad said.

"Well, in pretty much every spy or heist movie, the main character has to do a few things before pulling off the objective: they have to get help from a team of experts, they do reconnaissance on the area of interest, they try to find an inside person, someone who will tell them important information, and they have a plan or blueprint of their main objectives of what they want to accomplish," Paul said, using his free hand to illustrate his point.

"Okay, I see what you're saying. So you want me to 'apply like a spy'?" Chad put on his best debonair look and put his last words in air quotes.

Paul stopped for a moment and jabbed out his cane like he was fighting off an imaginary enemy, using his mouth to make sound effects. Chad laughed at the display. Once Paul had vanquished the invisible opponent, he grinned and said, "Exactly. You can do the exact same things as you're looking for the right opportunity, and company, to work for."

"How so?"

"Well, you start by getting help from lots of different sources. I'll continue to be a resource in your journey, but there are also so many other authors, leaders, and coaches that can help you along your path, some of whom I've already mentioned over the last few weeks," Paul said, resuming the hike.

Chad jotted down a few sentences in his ever-present notebook, then nodded and asked, "Okay, what else?" "There are so many different ways to do recon on the companies and opportunities you're looking at; some of the best of them are looking at anonymous reviews online, asking current and former employees what they think of the company, looking at their ratings for customer service, and also employee engagement surveys or awards if they have any.

"Take your time and use a legal pad or virtual document to write down your discoveries as you research, and don't forget to look at the company's website, not only to get a feel for who they are and what they value, but also to help you study for your interview."

Chad took a moment to bend down and pet Grace. "Yeah, I don't want what happened last time to happen next time, that's for sure."

"Your goal should be to find at least one person who's working within the organization you're looking at, and ask them some of the following questions:

"How do you like working here? What's the best part of your job?

What's the worst part of your job? Describe the culture of where you work. Do you enjoy working with your immediate supervisor and team, and if so, why?"

Chad jotted in his notebook and nodded. "Man, these are some good questions!"

Paul smiled. "The great thing is, you can ask anyone these questions to get an understanding of how they feel, and if you ask enough people, you can get a feel for how the company is as a whole. This 'ground truth' will help you know what employees are thinking and experiencing every day."

"This makes a lot of sense," Chad said, stepping over a small branch. "It seems like the people I know who are looking for jobs look for online postings and submit their applications without doing a ton of homework or research."

"It's true, Chad. Many people spend more time binge-watching the latest TV series than they do researching and planning out their next career move. As for the blueprint phase, it's vital for you to map out what your main objectives are in your research, and what's mission critical. Too often people focus on the job itself, the hours, or benefits to a current position. Those are all important, but let me suggest some things that I would argue are just as, if not more, important. Ask yourself:

"Does the company live out its mission statement and foster an atmosphere in which the workers support each other? When you step into one of the company's locations or when you interact with someone there, do you have positive feelings? Do the people seem happy doing what they're doing?"

"Wow," Chad said, shaking his head, "this is all really good, Paul, but I'm starting out here. I don't have any connections ... How can I get to know others?"

"You know, I've heard of plenty of different ways to grow your personal and professional network. I've never found much success in traditional networking groups, because referrals and connections based off obligation don't tend to go as far as real, organic relationships based on mutual interests."

"I see ... well, what's worked for you in connecting with others?" Chad asked, thinking of the massive business Paul had started.

"The best way to grow your network of contacts is to serve others, find new opportunities to volunteer with organizations that you're passionate about, and plug yourself into recreational groups. For instance, I had connected, hiked, and camped with my group of friends every month, and through that time together, we got to know each other. Unbeknownst to me, when the time was right, we had built a relationship based on our love for nature and helping each other. Long story short, we became friends first."

"I have been thinking about volunteering at the food bank. I know I have a ton going on, but I was reflecting on how much it meant to my family to receive support when things were tight for us," Chad said, rubbing the back of his neck.

"Chad, that's a great place to start! When you serve others, and get to do so around people who have that same desire for service, you'll develop some strong connections," Paul said.

"So," Chad said, his brow slightly furrowed, "I understand that will help me personally, but how will that help my job search?"

"Well, when you build relationships the way that I'm describing, you'll find that people want to help you in your personal and professional life, and that it won't feel forced. You, in turn, will want to point them toward opportunities and people that can help them grow as well," Paul said, pushing a rock with his cane and watching it skitter down the path ahead.

"I will tell you that there are certain types of people, people called Connectors, as described in Malcom Gladwell's book *The Tipping Point*. Gladwell talks about how there's a type of person who is naturally more outgoing and has a lot of acquaintances, through personal, professional, and recreational activities. But what makes them true Connectors is that they know enough about the people in their network to offer help and support to you, and will ask for your help and support, depending on the situation.

"Their main goal is doing good and finding and filling needs. For example, one of my good friends, Jenny, who works at a local credit union here in town, literally knows everyone. That's at least the joke, anyway. She's a true Connector, because she gets to know people and what they're about in order to help them as situations arise. She's someone I love to have people meet, not only because she's a great person, but because she truly enjoys connecting people and helping them," Paul said, pulling on Grace's leash gently so the dog came trotting by their side.

Chad's notebook page was full, and the sound of crackling paper filled the quiet trail as he turned the page to continue documenting Paul's words.

"Wow, this is good stuff! It sounds like I've got a lot of work to do! Do you mind if I recap?"

They were nearing the trailhead when Paul stopped to lean over and look. "It looks great, Chad! I can't wait to hear how you 'apply like a spy' to find the perfect opportunities that God has for you. I'll be praying for you, and I encourage you to do the same, seeking the Lord about what he wants you to do and where he wants you to look! This is your mission, if you choose to accept it. "

CHAPTER 12
YOUR BEST FOOT FORWARD

Even though Chad had never worked harder in his life, or had more stress put on him, he felt a renewed sense of energy and purpose, especially with the prospect of finally applying the degree he had strived for. His control on his expenses had reached their limits however, and he was sure he had tried every combination of ramen and tuna he could think of. He had lived on a shoestring budget many years before, when his father left, and he had learned from his mom how to coax the most he could out of his budget, but it wouldn't cut it if he had to continue paying for school.

Aiden's solicitations continued in frequency, whether it was in person or by text. It seemed like every time Chad turned around, Aiden was there, reminding him of the opportunity he wasn't taking and what would happen to his future if he decided to rat Aiden out. As finals were approaching, Aiden's urgency increased to a fevered pitch, pressuring him constantly.

On Monday morning, Chad had so many questions and so many updates for Paul he decided to text him. *Hey, Paul! Are you available for coffee tomorrow morning?*

Paul's response was punctual, and soon Chad had a time set in his phone for their talk at a downtown bakery, overlooking the lake.

~

As Chad rounded the corner, he spotted Paul already sitting outside at a table under the covered patio. The private bistro tables, colorful décor and smell of fresh pastries all put Chad at ease as he sat down. "Paul, it's good to see you!" Chad said. "I need to talk with you about something."

"It's good to see you too, Chad," Paul said, the crow's feet around his eyes compressing as he smiled. "What's going on?"

"It's just ... I ... I haven't been a hundred percent honest with you about what's been going on with me. About school, I mean." Chad looked down at the table.

"What do you mean?"

"Well, there's this guy, Aiden ..." Chad started. He began from the beginning, and explained in detail his relationship with Aiden, and everything that had happened since they met.

"Wow." Paul leaned back in his chair. "It must've been hard for you to experience that level of temptation and guilt."

"What do you mean by guilt? I didn't do anything wrong!" Chad said.

"You're right, you haven't, but you're acting as though you have," Paul said slowly. "You've been playing right into what Aiden wants, which is to continue to speak lies to you, to tempt you with what you think you need."

"You're right. I think I've been so afraid I would get in trouble, and though I know it isn't right, I've been tempted to take him up on his offer." Chad sighed. "I'm not sure what I should do, Paul, and I'm sorry for not sharing this with you sooner. It just felt too big, and ... do you have any advice for me?"

Paul thought for a moment, then said, "Chad, have you ever encountered a snake before?"

"A snake?" Chad tilted his head. "Yeah, when I was growing up there was one time we saw a snake on our back porch, sunning itself. Why?"

"There was one time when my son Charlie, who was maybe three years old, was playing in the grass in our backyard. As I looked over to check on him, I saw a snake lying next to him. Charlie was trying to pick it up by the tail. My reflexes kicked in, and I ran faster than I ever have before, or since, preparing to hurl myself toward the snake and the danger it posed to my young son. As I got within about five feet of the snake, I spotted a metal garden rake out of the corner of my eye. I grabbed it, and in one motion, slammed the rake over the top of the snake's head, cutting it clean off," Paul said, intensity in his voice.

"Paul, that's ... that's crazy, and kind of disgusting," Chad said, wrinkling his nose.

"I know my story is graphic, but the point is: you don't mess around with snakes. You don't try to grab them by the tail and gently move them. You cut off the snake by the head, and you don't play around with it or entertain its presence. Do you understand what I'm trying to say here, Chad?" Paul asked, folding his hands.

"Holy moly, Paul ... Aiden calls his program the 'Viper Protocol,'" Chad said with wide eyes. Paul simply nodded. "I think I know what to do, but I'm afraid of the consequences, and what they might do to my chances of graduation."

"The temptation you're facing won't take you where you want to go, Chad, I guarantee it. God always provides a way out, even when we fear what the consequences may be," Paul said.

"Thank you, Paul, you've given me a lot to think about here," Chad said.

"I'd encourage you to keep talking to God about this specific challenge in your life," Paul responded, smiling. "What else has been going on with you?"

"Well, I think I may have found two great opportunities at companies that could help me grow a lot! I used all your tips, and I've got some notes on both," Chad said, pulling out his spiral bound notebook and flipping through the pages, showing Paul. Paul's eyes shone with pride as Chad filled him in on all the details.

"Wow, Chad," Paul said, shaking his head, "those both sound great. You've done your homework!"

"Yeah, I'm pretty excited about both," Chad said, "but I don't want a repeat of last time I tried to apply ..."

A memory flashed through his mind, and he realized just how miserably he'd failed during his interview with Gary.

"Can you give me some advice on how to make sure I do it right?" he asked.

"Chad, I'm excited you're asking me about this! I was planning to cover some of this on Saturday, but I think we should talk about this today so you can present your best self! It's our ninth principle: **Your Best Foot Forward**," Paul said, his excitement rising with every word. "Presenting your best, authentic self, is something that takes some time and a little practice, but I'm going to give you some tips to help you, specifically when it comes to the workplace. For starters, can you tell me how you dressed for your interview with Gary recently?"

Chad listed his apparel. "Well, I wore a pair of jeans, a ball cap, a tee shirt ... I don't know, sneakers?"

"Okay," Paul said with a nod. "Now can you tell me what you wore at the last wedding you attended?"

"Hmm ..." Chad thought for a moment. "It would've been a few years back, when I went to my cousin's wedding. I wore a nice pair of slacks, a dress shirt, a tie, and I think a jacket of some sort for a while, at least until the dancing started."

Paul's eyebrows rose. "Why, Chad, I didn't know you knew how to 'bust a move,' as the kids say."

Chad facepalmed as Paul chuckled. "Seriously, though. Why didn't you just wear your jeans, tee shirt, and ball cap to the wedding?"

"I'm pretty sure I would be kicked out of the family if I did that!" Chad said, leaning back in his chair, a smile still on his face.

"I don't know about that. Do you see what I'm getting at here though, Chad? We dress our best at weddings to honor the bride and groom and their new beginning of life together. But here's the thing: the interview is our first step toward a new life in our careers. If we go into an establishment and we don't portray a healthy respect for it, we won't be successful. We want to present the best of who we are, and help represent our Father, even in the details.

"Here are some quick things to improve when it comes to appearance: always dress at least one level higher than you think is required for any meeting or interview, if you're walking into a new place, because it's important to look your best. For you this would mean nice dress shoes, slacks, a collared shirt, tie, and possibly a jacket. You may find you don't need a tie or jacket, but it's always easier to dress down after the fact."

Chad, his palm cramping from writing so fast, shook his hand for a moment. He was trying hard to catch every word Paul said. "I see ... I guess I've always just dressed the way everyone else around me does."

"If you dress for success, Chad, there is a higher level of confidence and purpose that comes when you look and feel professional. And since we're talking about how to present yourself, one of the best ways you can do that is by dropping off your resume or cover letter and any other important information in person, as well as applying online for the two positions you're looking at. This shows a higher level of initiative, and gives you more opportunities to meet key people in the organization.

"For example, one of the managers we have working for us currently at P.J. Outfitters, Dustin, had no experience working in retail. He did know how to work hard on the farm, and was willing to put himself out there. We took a chance on him, and I credit much of his success to his initiative. He was also dressed professionally when he came in, which caught everyone's attention from day one. The little things matter, including his handshake and professional resume." Paul took a moment to sip his coffee and take a bite of donut.

"Speaking of resume writing," Chad said, taking advantage of the break to pull out a sheet of paper from his backpack, "I have mine right here! I didn't update my resume for my most recent interview, which looking back I definitely should have. Would you mind looking over it real quick, and telling me what you think?"

Paul took the resume and took his time, reading it over before responding, "Chad, this looks good, but I think it needs a few things to be great. Your resume is a good opportunity for people to know what you've done, but more importantly, who you are. The best resumes bring in your mission statement, your strengths, why this opportunity is important to you, and specific examples of how you've been successful.

"Your resume tells a story; if you use it to just list off your skills and work experience, you're doing the reader a disservice. As a side note, make sure you're always changing the position and company with each resume submitted, along with the cover letter. It's an extra step, but worth it to help you stand above all the other hundreds of generic submissions companies receive."

Chad started jotting down notes, but then stopped and looked up at Paul. "Paul, I'm going to be honest. I'm scared at the thought of being interviewed. Talking to a large group, or one on one, I feel like I have to puff myself up," he said, "or be overconfident to get myself to actually do it."

"Chad, a recent study showed ninety-two percent (1) of adults fear something about the interviewing process. Our discussions on our last few hikes have been helping you see your authentic, true self. Once you see and are comfortable with who you are, you can present yourself in a real way to others."

Chad nodded his head and continued writing. "Okay, so how do I put that into practice?"

"My boy, that's exactly the word I was going to use: practice. Remember our baseball analogy from earlier, where we talked about how often you'd be able to hit the stop sign? You told me if you practiced hard for two weeks straight, you'd be able to get a lot better using your naturally dominant arm. You will never become comfortable sharing who you are, and what's important to you, without doing it regularly. In this case, I would highly recommend you record yourself answering common interview questions."

Chad stopped and lifted his head again, cocking it in confusion. "You mean like, set-up-a-tripod-with-my-phone recording?"

"Yes. We're normally our own toughest critic, and by watching yourself on video, you can ask yourself the following questions:

Was my answer true and authentic to who I really am, or was I pretending to be someone else?

Did I answer the question clearly?

Did I answer the question directly, and did I pull in examples from my life that highlight my strengths and heart for others?

What things did I like, and what did I dislike about my conversation?

"Now some simple tips to clinch the interview: be sure to make eye contact with the interviewer, keep your tone friendly and confident, and be aware of your facial expressions and non-verbal communication. For instance, be sure to smile!"

Chad finished writing and said, "Paul, this sure feels like a lot."

"Chad, there's a quote from Mark Udall that says, 'You never climb a mountain by accident—it has to be intentional.' This holds true for the mountain of interviewing and presenting yourself. You have to put in the time, work, and heart-level focus to display the best of who you are," Paul said, rubbing his chin.

"I would recommend you video and do these mock interviews with yourself once per day. Additionally, I'd love it if you'd send me the first few videos you do, so I can review them and give you some feedback."

"I can do that," Chad said. "I know this won't feel natural at all at first, but I'm sure it'll help a lot when I interview for either of these jobs."

"But now comes the most important part," Paul said, leaning forward intently, "the part that ties in your resume writing, your dress, presenting yourself to people, and interviewing: prayer. Every day, pray over your interactions, your resume, your self-presentation, your interviews. Pray out loud to your Father in heaven, ask him to bless you and your work. This is a powerful way to make him real to you. By bringing him into every detail."

"Wow..." Chad looked down, then back up again. "Can we do that now? Pray, I mean?"

"You bet, Chad," Paul said, closing his eyes and bowing his head while Chad did the same. "Father, thank you for creating Chad and helping him see his true value and worth. We thank you for revealing the steps he needs to take on this journey and that he's receiving your direction. Help him continue in love and pursuit of you throughout this process. Amen."

(1 - 2013 Job Interview Anxiety Survey)

CHAPTER 13
TELL YOUR STORY

"I don't quite understand what you're saying here, Chad," Gary said, folding his hands on his desk.

"I'm concerned, sir," Chad said, sitting straight up in his chair and looking Gary in the eyes. "Yesterday, Micah shoved my coworker Thomas into a pile of laundry on account of him 'looking at him wrong.' This type of behavior has been going on for weeks now. He's kept us hours past our scheduled shifts for various infractions, and told us not to put it on our time card, threatening more punishment if we did."

With a stern and condescending tone, Gary said, "Now, Chad, I know you and Micah haven't had the best relationship, but I feel like you're being a bit over dramatic."

"Sir, I understand that Micah and I have not seen eye to eye, and honestly I haven't treated him well at all in the past. I request that you ask some of my coworkers what's been happening, so that these concerns can be addressed. I care too much about them to not say something," he said.

Gary looked up at the clock and saw that it was two minutes till the start of the shift. "It looks like your shift's about to start. I'd recommend getting going so you're not late."

With that, Gary got up and left the office. Chad took a deep breath, sighed, and took a moment to thank the Lord, praying that things would get better from here.

When he opened the door to leave, he found Gary exchanging quick, whispered words with a livid Micah. Nodding to Chad, Gary turned on his heel and left Chad alone with the unchained beast of Micah's rage.

"You tried to get me fired!" Micah almost yelled, pushing Chad's chest and slamming him into the wall.

"Micah, I—"

"Shut up!" Micah raised his fist and punched, but Chad was able to move out of the way and Micah's hand hit the wood-paneled wall with an ominous pop. Micah grabbed his wrist and curled over, gritting his teeth.

"You're dead, Chad," he said, walking slowly away. "Dead."

The next day, Micah decided to exact his revenge, but not in a way Chad expected at all.

Chad was cleaning his workstation and gathering his things to leave when Micah walked up, his gritted teeth a poor excuse for a smile. "Chad, I've decided how I'm going to get you back."

Chad mentally prepared himself.

"I'm going to make sure you get fired. And the way I'm going to do that is to embarrass you in front of the entire plant. You're going to run the safety meeting next Friday. Everyone's going to watch you utterly fail, and when that happens, I'll have plenty of justification for letting you go," Micah sneered.

Chad felt the old anger from his past trying to crawl its way to the surface, but his knowledge that he was accountable to God quelled any selfish desire to lash out at Micah.

I've been praying and turning the situation over to you, God. Praying that it would improve, and all I can see is that it's getting worse. I don't know what you're doing here, but I trust you'll be with me.

"What do you want me to present?" Chad asked.

Micah's eyebrows furrowed over dark, smoldering coals. "You'll be going over our hazardous materials and floor safety procedures. Gary told me how much you screwed up your interview with him, so I can't wait to see how badly you butcher this!"

Micah laughed, turned around and slithered out of the building.

"I didn't realize how steep of a climb this would be!" Chad said.

"Do you mean our hike up Mica Peak today, or the mountains you're facing in your work life?" Paul asked.

"Both." Chad chuckled, sweat beading on his brow. "But it's not all bad news. I pursued both job opportunities we talked about last week, and I have an in-person interview set up next week, which I'm super excited about!"

"Chad, that's great! I've genuinely enjoyed watching your interview videos. I can see your confidence growing, and I encourage you to keep practicing so you feel ready to do your very best in your interview," Paul said, his breath even and unlabored as he climbed up the trail with seeming ease.

"It sounds crazy to say, but I'm almost done with school," Chad said, shaking his head. "I only have two weeks left, and I feel like I'm on the home stretch. The biggest mountain I'm climbing at the moment is the safety meeting."

Chad went over the events of the last few days, including Micah's assignment.

"It sounds like you've decided to take this challenge head-on," Paul said, grinning.

Chad returned his grin. "I feel like I owe it to the guys I work with, and myself, to tackle this head-on. But I might need a little help." Chad caught himself. "More like a lot of help."

The pair laughed as they strained to climb up a steeper path. After a few more minutes of climbing they came to a flat plateau of grass and decided to take a break, giving Grace a rest and them the excuse to soak up the sun. Paul used a large rock to lower himself to the ground, looked at it for a moment, then began to speak.

"You know, this rock reminds me of a story. One day, God came down and spoke to a man. He gave him an assignment, and said 'See this boulder before you? I want you to push this boulder.' The man was small and wiry, but he tried to push the boulder for hours, to the point of exhaustion.

"The next day, he got up and tried to move the boulder again, pushing from multiple different angles. He did this day after day, week after week, until finally months later, he slumped down and gave up. He cried out to God, saying, 'God, you asked me to move this boulder, and I've faithfully followed you for months now, attempting to do just that, and nothing's happened!'

"With love in his voice, God said, 'I didn't ask you to move this boulder; I asked you to push against it. Look at your body, and how it's changed. Look at the muscles and determination that you've developed.'"

Paul paused, then looking Chad in the eyes, said, "You see, Chad, many times we focus on the circumstances changing when God's heart is for us to change in the process. In short, it's the process that changes us, not the results."

Chad laughed and shook his head. "I've certainly had a lot of boulders in my life, then."

"You're right, Chad, and Micah's just one of them. How much stronger we would all be if we decided to ask how God wanted to change us, as we push on the boulders in our lives, instead of wishing they were never there in the first place."

Paul looked over to see Chad furiously writing down notes. After a moment, Paul asked, "Are you ready to keep going, and push against the boulder of public speaking? It's our tenth principle: **Tell Your Story.**"

Chad finished writing, looked up at Paul, and answered, "Yes. Yes I am."

"I'm going to give you the five secrets of presenting to a group. Starting with number one: Practice. You need to know your subject inside and out, and practice sharing it as much as possible before your presentation. In this case, practicing your presentation one to two times per day will be vital to helping you feel comfortable and confident. I recommend using small, three-by-five cards to jot down important notes, and to help keep you on track."

"Who do I present to?" Chad asked, "I don't live with anybody."

"Do you happen to have a potted plant?"

Chad furrowed his eyebrows and cocked his head. "Umm ... yes?"

"What type of plant is it?"

"Uh, a ficus, I think."

Paul put a finger to his lips. "Hmm ... how about Micus? Micus the Ficus. Plants make a great audience. They don't object, talk back, or make any derogatory comments," Paul said, his face dead serious. Then he cracked a smile, putting Chad at ease. "I'm joking, of course. That phone you used to film yourself works, although a live audience of friends or family will help you get to the stage where you're feeling comfortable presenting. I'd love to hear your presentation, maybe Thursday morning, since you said the big day is Friday?"

"That would be great!" Chad said enthusiastically. "What are the other four?"

"The next one is: Finding your person. Whenever you're presenting to a group, pick out one person that you can use to help gauge the effectiveness of your presentation. I suggest finding someone closer up, in the first few rows, who naturally is more outwardly expressive. They'll give you head nods when they understand or agree, or furrow their brow and tilt their head if they don't quite get it. Think of them as your temperature gauge, helping you know where you're at."

"I think I might know a couple of people at the plant like that," Chad said, nodding. "What else?"

"As you're presenting, I want you to practice what Stacy Henkie (2) described as the 'Arc and Park.' The goal is to move in a semicircle, facing your audience, and stop at certain points along the way to keep your audience's interest and help them stay engaged." Paul walked in a semicircle, displaying this in real life as he explained.

"Ooh, I get it," Chad said, nodding.

"Since we're talking about 'Arcing,' our fourth tip focuses on the A.R.C. model when it comes to giving a speech. The acronym stands for, attention, relevant, and compelling. The goal is to increase your audience's interest as time moves forward."

Paul described a small diagram, which Chad drew in his notebook.

"Your goal with 'attention,' from the beginning, is to try to capture them in less than ten seconds. Startling comments, jokes, or even nonverbal movements can help accomplish this goal. Next, you need to be 'relevant.' You want to communicate how your message will impact the lives of your audience. It has to resonate with them on a personal level. And last, it needs to be 'compelling.' It needs to be a summary of what you've presented, a call to action. People must be moved to make decisions in their lives because of what you've said." Paul waited a moment for Chad to find a blank page to write on.

Chad shook his head. "And to think I was planning on reading the policy word-for-word in front of everyone."

Paul smiled. "And last, but not least: the goal is to move your audience from where they started to someplace new. The very best way to accomplish this is to make them think, laugh, or cry as part of your presentation. When any message is personalized and internalized by your audience, the effectiveness of your message skyrockets. Even though in this situation, Micah's chosen to give you this platform to see you fail, I believe you'll succeed when you communicate the importance of safety, and more importantly, caring for the people you work with every day."

"You're right, Paul," Chad said. "I tend to see things like safety meetings as something I have to do, and I don't connect with why the message might be important for me to hear and understand. I'm actually getting excited to put this presentation together, and share it with my team!"

"Hmm. Sounds like your heart may be changing toward the folks you work with," Paul said, clearly pleased.

"Heh, yeah," Chad said, rubbing the back of his neck. "I'm starting to grow closer to some of the guys I work with, and enjoying the time that we spend together, even though conditions have been hard with Micah."

Paul nodded. "With these tools, and with strength and inspiration from your heavenly Father, I know you're going to do an incredible job!"

(2 Stacy Hanke: 1st Impression Consulting)

CHAPTER 14
PUT TO THE TEST

C had had to keep deleting videos from his phone to make enough room for all the new ones he was creating. *I don't think I've ever talked this much in my life!*

He had spent the beginning of the week in frenzied preparation for his interviews on Monday and Wednesday. When he walked in the doors, he felt prepared to show what kind of person he was. But he still arrived at both interviews nervous and was at times uncertain if his answers hit the mark.

He had to admit that the process went a thousand times better than his previous interview experiences. He was basing this on his own confidence going into the interviews and the non-verbal approval he received during and after his sit-downs.

After the interviews came the preparation for the safety meeting. He started asking himself, *Why should my coworkers care about the safety meeting?* If he was honest, he had feigned interest during the monthly affair, hosted by Gary. These were dry, boring times for everyone involved. Even Gary seemed to get bored with what he had to say.

However, Chad was determined to break the cycle. He spent hours of his time figuring out how to make his speech relevant and real for his coworkers, and took time during his work days talking with them, asking what was important to them, and he felt it paid off when he looked at the finished product.

Chad decided to send this version to Paul to get his feedback, and was given lots of encouragement and affirmation to ramp up his energy at the end of his speech. Paul also made sure to mention connecting with the audience in a few key ways. Chad estimated he had practiced his interviewing and presentation at least forty times in five days, and he was convinced Micus the Ficus was much more inspired than before.

~

When Friday morning rolled around, Chad was ready. He had arrived twenty minutes early, so he could set up the training room and have copies of the policy printed and set out.

Thomas, his coworker, had been waiting in the parking lot when Chad arrived, and he was more than willing to help him set up shop. Soon, when people were filing into the room, Chad spotted one face in particular he wasn't expecting. He nudged Thomas and pointed. "Hey, Tom, that's our general manager."

Thomas squinted for a moment, then his eyes grew wide and he grabbed Chad's shoulder with shock. "She's real?"

It was all Chad could do to keep from laughing out loud. The GM was based out of the Seattle area, a good five-hour drive from Coeur d'Alene, and they didn't see her very often, especially at the safety meetings. Nevertheless, Chad was ready to take on the added pressure. He knew this meeting had changed in significance for him as he started to genuinely care more about the protection and securing of both his coworkers and his clients. This would be a defining moment in his career and personal journey, no matter how it turned out.

Chad noticed a quiet nervousness among the group when they were at last assembled and ready. At exactly seven fifty-nine, Micah sauntered into the room and took a seat near Gary and the GM. He sat, arms crossed, his mouth smirking and eyes glaring in Chad's direction.

As Chad walked up to the front of the room, he silently prayed, *God, please give me the strength and the words to say to these men to convey your love to them.*

Chad's voice started out a bit shaky as he addressed the group. "Good morning, everyone. Thank you for being here."

A scoff came from Micah's seat. "It's a required safety meeting, Chad. Everybody has to be here."

Gary's head turned and he looked at Micah with a disapproving glare. Micah got the hint: no more outbursts moving forward.

Chad turned to the dry erase board and wrote out the question, *Why is safety important to you?*

"As we get started, it's vital for us to understand why we're talking about safety this morning. Sure, it's required," he nodded at Micah, "but I have a feeling it goes much deeper than that for many of us."

There were a few moments of silence. Chad started to get worried, but then he remembered that Paul had mentioned to pull out friends from the crowd, people he could engage with when needed.

"Thomas, can you help start us off with this one? Why is safety important to you?"

Thomas rubbed his chin for a moment. "Yeah ... I think safety is important to me because if things aren't secured, our jobs won't be either. Like, the government will shut us down or something."

A third of the room chuckled at this remark, much to the obvious annoyance of Micah.

"You're right, Tom," Chad said. "We can't have work here without protection being top-priority."

He then asked a few other coworkers why it was important to them, and jotted their answers down on the board. "So, to summarize, we have the ability to have our jobs and keep our doors open, it is company policy, and we don't want to get fired. These are good, but do you mind if I add one?"

Chad took a red marker and wrote in big letters, *Because we care for each other*, and underlined the words. "Brian, I've seen you stay late to help Jonathan the Janitor with cleaning the windows. Kyle, I know you've sorted Thomas's sack for him on multiple occasions. Thomas, you've kept the break room stocked with your mom's homemade cookies, which is the greatest act of kindness any of us could ask for."

The room rang with laughter at the truth behind the statement. When all was quiet again, Chad continued, "You see, guys, the care we show for each other can and should be reflected in the safety of our workplace as we pay attention to policies and procedures and look out for one another. Steven, would you mind reading the first section of our hazardous materials policy?"

Steven gave a half smile and, in his deep baritone voice, began to read. Somehow, the soothing quality made the boring jargon sound intriguing.

"Thank you, Steven. Man, you could read the phone book and make it sound interesting."

Chuckles and nods of agreement filled the room. "But seriously, I appreciate you highlighting how we can help protect each other here at WeSort4U. For the sake of time, I'd like for each of us to read the entire policy with what we've talked about in mind, and connect with Gary before the day is over, to share what you've learned and to sign the Corporate Acknowledgement Statement. Does that sound okay to you, Gary?"

Gary looked at him, stunned, and nodded his head, "Y-yes, that works great." It normally took him at least a few days to wrangle everyone into giving their half-hearted consent to the monthly safety highlight.

With that, Chad said, "Thank you guys for participating today. I care too much about you guys to see any of you getting injured on the job, and I know many of you feel the same way. Have a good rest of your day."

Micah was visibly shaking with anger. With clenched fists, he stood and was one of the first to walk out of the room. A few of Chad's coworkers came up to him and thanked him for leading one of the best safety meetings they'd ever attended.

Once they'd left, Gary approached Chad with the GM by his side and said, "Chad, you did well today."

Chad was a bit taken aback, since Gary didn't give out public praise often. "Thank you, sir!"

"I don't believe you've met our general manager yet, have you? Chad, this is Kelly. Kelly, meet Chad."

Chad reached out his hand to shake Kelly's. "Ma'am, it's great to meet you."

With a stern look, Kelly said, "Chad, I've never seen a safety meeting quite like that one."

The blood drained a bit out of Chad's face, and as he was about to speak, Kelly broke out into a grin and said, "It was one of the best ones I've ever seen!"

Chad let out a laugh that was partially a sigh of relief. "Oh, thank you, ma'am!"

"It was better than some I've conducted," she continued. They connected for a few minutes before Chad asked, "How long will you be in town for?"

Kelly's tone became more serious. "I'm not quite sure how long my visit will be this time around. Gary and I have a few things to discuss."

Chad noticed Gary looked more concerned than anything at this remark. "But I'd like to connect with you again before I leave town, Chad," she finished. "Thank you for sharing today, and putting your heart into that presentation."

As Chad left to get to class, since his shift didn't start till three, he felt an amazing amount of gratitude bubbling up in his spirit to Paul and to God for helping him get so far in his journey. He thought back to a few weeks ago, and knew that none of this would have been possible without their help. He couldn't wait to recount the events to Paul.

Chad pulled into the school's parking lot, shifted into park, and got out of his car, noticing his near-empty gas gauge. He'd have to put another five dollars in it before heading into work.

He shouldered his backpack and was about to head in when he heard a shout. "Hey! Chad! Wait up a second!"

Aiden was rapidly catching up to him, riding his slick black Onewheel. He braked and got off in one fluid motion in front of Chad. He knew in that instant that this conversation would be another defining moment for him. As Aiden opened his mouth, Chad blurted out, "I'm not doing it!"

As soon as the words left his lips, Chad felt an immense sense of relief, but also a sense of nervousness.

"Then you're dumber than I thought, Chad," Aiden said, a dark scowl on his face. "I offered you the opportunity to live like a king as you finish your time here. Without me, you'll finish out your college career like a rat in a dumpster."

With that, Aiden stalked off, calling over his shoulder, "And don't even think about telling Prof. Simmons about our arrangement, or I'll make sure you go down with me!"

As Aiden disappeared through the doors, Chad sighed, taking a deep breath. *I know what I gotta do.*

Chad entered the class and elected not to sit in his usual spot next to Aiden, but right where no one wanted to sit: The Front Row. He tried to focus on the lecture the entire time by taking notes, but found himself distracted by what he knew had to come next. His thoughts were consumed with the impending conversation with Professor Simmons. He ran through all the possible scenarios, trying to imagine how this would all play out; he could focus on nothing else until he heard the sound of the bell.

As students were filing out the door, Chad stayed behind. He looked up long enough to see Aiden walking down the stairs from the back of the room, glaring and mouthing, "Don't even think about it," doubling Chad's internal anxiety. With sweaty palms and a nervous shake, he walked over to Prof. Simmons's desk. As he approached, the teacher had his head down, adding notes to his now-completed lecture.

"Professor Simmons?" Chad asked tentatively.

Without looking up, the professor responded in a flat tone. "Yes, Chad?"

Is this guy even human? Chad wondered. His mechanical movements and precision, combined with his perfectly styled hair and dress, conveyed the impression that order and structure meant everything to him.

"I ... I think that there's been some cheating going on, sir."

At the mention of the word cheating, the professor stopped writing, placed his pen down on his desk, and slowly raised his head. He leaned forward and clasped his hands together. "I know that, Chad."

Chad was taken aback. "You-you know that people are cheating? Professor, I promise I'm not a part of it."

"Well, that's yet to be determined, but the data suggests you haven't been involved up to this point," he said, nodding his head.

"I'm sorry, I don't understand."

"You see, Chad, I'm a man who studies numbers and outcomes. Every year, with every class, I carefully study student's test scores, their participation, and their attentiveness during my lectures. What I've found is that none of us can have the desired outcome that we want without putting in the necessary components to make it happen."

Chad scratched his head. "Professor, can you clarify that a bit more?"

"Based on my analysis, and how I structure my class, I know within a 98% margin of error who is cheating in my class and when they start. There are certain classmates of yours who will fail this course, and some likely to be expelled for it, but up till this moment, you haven't been one of them," the Professor explained.

"How could you possibly know all that?" Chad was amazed.

"Well, when the cheating started in my class, you got a D on your test. And since then, your grades have slowly improved, including the quality of your overall work. It's not hard to see the difference when you study the facts like I do. From the data I've gathered, and my own observations, something has changed for you. You were headed toward failing this class, but if your current trend holds, you'll likely finish with a passing grade.

You've applied yourself, and removed negative variables that hindered you when you first started this course. I no longer see you sleeping, making conversation, or zoning out when I'm teaching. You also chose today to move from the back row to the front row and remove yourself from one specific negative variable."

Chad took this all in for a moment. *He's talking about Aiden, and cutting off the head of the snake!* "Sir, if you knew there was cheating going on the whole time, why would you allow it?"

Professor Simmons's expression was stern. "Chad, my course is one of the most difficult for students to pass. I know that the temptation to cheat is always present. I always wait and see who decides to give in, and who decides to hold firm, and I don't turn in my conclusions to the dean until the week of finals every semester. This gives me the most data possible to present my findings."

"Wow," Chad shook his head. "I had no idea."

"Most students don't. But now that you have this knowledge, I trust that you, and hopefully many of your classmates, will continue to finish this class with integrity, respect for this institution, and yourself."

Chad was a few minutes early for his three o'clock shift, and when he walked into the plant he expected the normal sights and sounds of machines running and sorters sorting. What he saw instead was a scene of chaos: all work had stopped as Micah burst from Gary's office yelling at the top of his lungs, with Gary and Kelly right behind him.

"You're calling me a thief and a liar?" Micah shouted, spinning around and pointing a finger at the approaching pair.

Kelly calmly walked toward Micah and in a low tone said, "Micah, I need you to calm down and come back into the office, so we can continue our conversation. Things aren't adding up, and I need your help in understanding what's going on."

Micah darted forward, his face beet red, and screamed right in Kelly's face, "You want to know what's going on? I'll tell you what's going on! Gary's been stealing from the company, and he roped me into it!"

There was an audible gasp around the plant floor, and Gary looked like he'd been sucker punched. Kelly turned to look at him, questioning with her eyes. Gary started shaking his head, "No, I—"

Kelly put her hand up, stopping both Gary and Micah. In a commanding, resounding voice she said, "Micah, Gary, I need the two of you to walk outside of this plant *right now*, where I hope we'll have an actual conversation."

Both Gary and Micah solemnly exited the building, Kelly following behind them. She paused for a moment, looking at Chad, who was standing by the exit. "Chad, can I trust you to help the team get back to work while I'm talking to Gary and Micah?"

Chad nodded, and said, "Yes ma'am!"

As Kelly exited the building, everyone gathered around Chad in a circle, all asking different questions:

"What just happened?"

"Do you think Gary's really been stealing?"

"Are we going to be rid of both of those guys?"

Chad spoke with conviction and authority. "Guys, I don't know what just happened here, or what the outcome will be, but I do hope that Kelly can get to the bottom of whatever's going on. I know that many of us have had a difficult time with Micah and Gary, but it's my hope that we won't rush to any judgment, and I pray that the truth will be revealed in this situation." Chad took a deep breath, looking at the skeptical and angry faces of the workers around him, and knew it was time to make a bold choice.

"You guys have all seen a change in me these past few weeks. I've treated many of you poorly in the past, and I didn't care about or consider any of you. I was too focused on myself. But God's changed that. He's the one who deserves the credit for every good thing in our lives. If he can change me, I know he can use this situation to help Gary and Micah. I don't know what the outcome will be, but I'd like to pray for the two of them and Kelly before we start our shift. Are you guys okay with that?"

He saw many solemn nods, a few blank stares, and a couple 'whatever' shrugs. Chad knew that today would help define the rest of his career, but he had no idea it would look like this.

CHAPTER 15
LOVE THE PROCESS

"Chad, I can't believe we didn't think of doing this sooner!" Paul said, his bare feet sinking slowly into the sand with every step. They had decided to bring their coffee to the beach and walk while they talked.

"I loved our hike on Saturday, and I'm going to miss hiking with you every weekend." Chad found himself choking with a bit of emotion he wasn't expecting.

Paul smiled and stopped for a moment. "Chad, this will not be our last hike, I can promise you that. I'm so proud of you, and excited to see your growth. I know a lot has happened, and it probably feels like there's a lot you can't control."

"Well, yeah, honestly," Chad said, rubbing the back of his neck. "I'm still waiting to hear back from both of my interviews, the ones from last week. I have no idea what's going to happen with Gary and Micah. Last I heard, they were still on leave. I literally have enough to cover my expenses for the month of August, and pay for my diploma. But my job and pay situation will need to change quickly," he rambled on, glancing at Paul. "I ... I feel conflicted, I guess. On the one hand, I have peace. God knows what's best for me and will do what he sees is right. On the other hand, I have this gnawing anxiety. I have no idea if either of the jobs I interviewed for will accept me, and my job at WeSort4U may even be in jeopardy."

"Chad, I can relate to what you're feeling and how you're thinking. There have been so many times in my life when I've questioned the path I'm on and where it will lead me. Your experiences tie perfectly into our eleventh principle: **Love the Process.** I can tell you, with all the confidence in my heart, there is one path. One way the Father is leading you in this life. You never have to go it alone; not anymore. God has already gone ahead of you, lovingly showing you the next steps to take."

"Wait a minute ..." Chad said, his eyes slowly widening. "This is just like our hikes! You've led me on more difficult and challenging routes and helped build up my stamina and strength over time. There were so many times I wasn't sure what was coming up around the next bend, or where you were taking me, but as we've been hiking together I've grown to trust you more. That's what you're talking about, isn't it?"

Paul stopped and grabbed Chad's shoulder, the biggest smile Chad had ever seen on his face. "Chad, that's exactly what we've been doing here! You see, you are learning things I wish I had known thirty years ago, and applying lessons in your own life that people in their seventies and eighties still haven't learned!"

After hearing these words, Chad's fear and anxiety began to melt away, and he grew more excited. As they continued to walk, Chad was thoughtful for a moment. Then he asked, "What happens when I get to the top of the mountain? I mean, what happens when I have the career I want, the income I need, and I reach the top?"

"Chad, you've asked a very important question, one that deserves the right setting to answer. I'd like to give you my thoughts about this during our next hike."

Chad's shoulders slumped a bit. "Are you really going to make me wait a week?"

Paul smirked a bit and nodded knowingly. "I promise it'll be worth the wait. I can't think of a better time or place for that conversation."

Chad resigned himself to the fact he wouldn't get his question answered today. As they were headed back to their cars, Paul asked, "By the way, when does your mom come into town for graduation?"

Chad's eyes got big as he said, "Oh my gosh, she flies in next week!"

"Chad, that's wonderful! Can you do me a favor and give me her contact information? I need her help to plan a graduation surprise for someone." Paul winked slyly.

CHAPTER 16
REACHING THE MOUNTAINTOP

That Saturday, Chad got up with the sun and drove for an hour to reach his final hiking destination with Paul: Arid Peak. He had lots of anticipation and nervousness for the last hike of his course. He was excited to tell him everything that had happened in the past few days, and he was ready to take on the most challenging hike of their twelve weeks together.

Paul arrived with Grace, and they had barely begun when Chad launched in, "Paul, I feel like I've had an entire week in just three days! I officially completed my finals yesterday, and after talking to Mrs.B, she confirmed that after today I'll have enough credits to graduate!"

Paul looked at him out of the corner of his eye. "You've got to make it up and down the mountain first, before you get a passing grade from me."

Chad laughed. "Challenge accepted."

"I'm so proud of you for sticking with it," Paul said, "and finishing strong. That was a pretty big mountain to climb."

"It's pretty incredible how much my heart and attitudes have shifted, when it comes to school and work ... oh, speaking of work! I got two job offers yesterday!" Chad said.

Paul jumped off the trail a little and pumped his fist in celebration,

"Yes! Chad, that's amazing! God is so good! So you're telling me both of the places you interviewed offered you a position?"

Grace barked at the activity, and Chad bent over to scratch her ear. "Well, not exactly. See, I went to work on Wednesday and got a call from one of the jobs. They told me no, and I was feeling pretty down for a couple days. I mean, I had one more shot at the other one, right? Then yesterday, I was getting ready for work, praying to God, asking him for his will to be done, and I got a call from the local credit union! They said they wanted to offer me the job!"

"Why didn't you tell me right away?" Paul said, a little incredulous.

"You're not the only one who can set up surprises," Chad said, smiling.

Paul smiled back, then a look of confusion crossed his face. "Wait a moment. You told me one job said no, and the credit union said yes. So, how did you get two offers then?"

Chad nodded, "Yeah, that's the crazy thing. See, I asked for twenty-four hours to think about it, and went into work, fully intending to give my two-week notice, when Kelly called me into the office ..."

～

"Do you know why I've asked you here today, Chad?" Kelly asked, folding her hands on her desk.

Chad knew in the back of his mind that Kelly was staying longer than she intended to, probably putting strain on her and her family, but appreciated her leadership in a time when so many things were up in the air.

"No ma'am," Chad said, shifting a bit in his seat.

"I wanted to let you know that both Gary and Micah are no longer employed at WeSort4U."

Chad couldn't help the shocked look on his face at this news. Just a few weeks ago, he would've responded with vengeful happiness. But instead, today, he felt sorrow for them and hoped that the situation would help be a turning point in their lives. "I'm sorry to hear that, ma'am, I am."

Kelly looked almost vindicated at the response and nodded. "Chad, I had a feeling you would respond that way. I too wish Gary and Micah well. Out of respect to them, I can't go into the details of what happened. I can tell you that my goal and vision is to have leaders working for us here at this plant, and all across our company, who believe in our core values and care for our people. Leaders like you, Chad."

At this, Chad lifted his head in surprise. "Like me, ma'am? What do you mean?"

"Chad, as I've been here for almost two weeks, I've had the opportunity to interview everyone here in this plant. I've asked each and every one of them who helps encourage them and who they look up to, who inspires them to work hard. I also heard about how you rallied everyone together after the incident with Gary and Micah on the floor, and turned what could've been a very toxic and chaotic situation into an opportunity for growth. Since I've also been here on site, I've had an opportunity to dive deeper into the metrics, and noticed that the plant's efficiency and service standards have increased exponentially. Many of the men here point to your encouragement and help on the floor as one of the major factors."

At this, Chad sat back in his chair and said, "Wow. I-I don't know what to say. Thank you, ma'am. If I'm honest, I feel like I've just been focusing on loving those around me, and just trying to give the very best while I'm here."

"Well, Chad, I need leaders like you, and I'd like to offer you the position of operations manager, if you'd be willing to accept it."

"Wait, you mean Gary's position? Running the whole plant?" Chad's voice rose in pitch a bit as he tried to comprehend. "I ... I wasn't expecting ... to be transparent with you, I was planning on giving my two-week notice today."

Now it was Kelly's turn to look a bit shocked. "Oh... I see."

Chad rubbed the back of his neck. "Yeah, I ... with everything going on here, and me graduating from college, I've been interviewing and was offered a job, before coming on shift."

Kelly sat back, contemplatively saying, "That makes sense. May I ask, have you accepted this new position yet?"

"Well, no, actually. I asked them to give me twenty-four hours to think about it," Chad said, leaning forward a bit and using his hands to illustrate his point.

"Chad, I'm going to ask that you consider staying on here at WeSort4U. I know it hasn't been your vision and I would understand if you decided to leave. But I feel like there's a lot of work to be done here at this location, and I'd feel honored to have you be a part of that. My goal would be to help you grow as a leader, and help you guide your coworkers in a positive and loving way."

Chad and Kelly discussed the role, pay, and benefits, and at the end of their conversation Chad said, "Wow, Kelly, you've given me a lot to think about. I'd like to run this by my mentor, who I'm connecting with tomorrow morning. Can I call you tomorrow afternoon with my decision?"

"You bet," Kelly said. "I want you to know that I will support you no matter what you decide, and I appreciate you taking a real look at this opportunity. I know that your experience working for us has been ... less than ideal. But I hope with your help we can change that."

Kelly stood, shook Chad's hand and thanked him.

"And that's pretty much what happened," Chad said as they continued up the steep incline.

Paul shook his head. "God is so good, and surprises us in so many specific ways. Chad, your character and heart-level change has created an opportunity for you that previously didn't exist. It sounds like you've got a pretty big decision to make."

"Yeah, I'm not sure which opportunity to choose. What would you do?"

"This is a decision that I can't influence. My recommendation to you is to spend some time after our hike writing down the pros and cons of each opportunity, both in the short and the long term. After doing that, I would ask the Lord what path he wants you to walk down," Paul said, leaning on his cane to traverse a large rock.

"It's so crazy that there's two opportunities in front of me when I only needed one. Both of them will more than pay for my expenses and allow me to pay down my debt quickly!" Chad said.

"That's so true, Chad. What does your mom have to say about this?"

Chad smiled and said, "Oh, her thoughts were pretty similar to yours. She said she loves me and will support me whatever way she can. Speaking of support ... I just wanted to say thank you for surprising her with a week's stay at the resort. She said her room over-looks the lake and she enjoys watching the sunset each evening. My mom doesn't get the chance to do things like that often, and I know she loves it."

Paul grinned, "I'm glad to hear it. I was hoping you two would be willing to join me for dinner this evening. We'll have a lot to celebrate."

"I would love that, Paul. You know, I realized the other day that if you wanted to, you could've gotten me a job at P.J. Outfitters, or paid for my school, or paid off my debt, but you didn't," Chad said, looking ahead.

Paul stopped for a moment, then continued up the trail. "It's true, Chad. I've been extremely blessed, and I could've done any of those things."

Chad paused, emotion rising up within. "You didn't ... you chose to give me something much more valuable. You chose to give me your time, and your love, and your wisdom. You chose to give me the best of who you are, and to share the only real hope that exists in this life. You've given me more than I could ever repay you for. You even gave up a three-week trip to the Holy Lands for me."

Paul's eyes widened. "How did you..."

Chad put his hand up. "Mrs. B slipped up and mentioned it while we were talking about my graduation requirements. She's normally as tight-lipped as you can get, but she mentioned how important that trip was to you."

Paul nodded. "It's true ... It's a trip my wife and I had always talked about, one that we wanted to do together. I'd been planning it for a long time."

"You would give ... why did you give that up for me?" Chad's voice rose and cracked a bit.

"I want to talk more about that, Chad, but can we wait until we reach the summit?" Paul asked tentatively.

Chad shook his head, "I've got to wait for this and the answer to my question from Tuesday?"

Paul laughed, "This is a perfect time to answer your mountain question, with our twelfth and final principle: **Reaching the Mountaintop**; we're nearly to the summit."

Chad had hardly noticed how strenuously they had been working. But now that he thought about it, his brow and shirt were sweaty, his legs were starting to ache, and his feet were sore as they were reaching the peak.

"One of my favorite speakers, Dean Grazioni, says 'God gives us legs for a reason. Once you summit and reach the top of the mountain, you climb another mountain.' God always equips us for the journey ahead, when we allow him to.

"As you move into this new phase, as you move into a new career, it's so important to look back from time to time and see the mountains you've climbed. It's also important to recognize the valleys and know that they serve a purpose as well.

"These mountaintop experiences, like what you're about to enjoy for this season, should be cherished. I'm going to encourage you to continue to invest in your relationships with others and with God, and to never stop growing. Your capacity in this life will always be determined by what I just shared with you," Paul said. He realized that Chad was a few steps behind, and looked back to see him taking notes.

Chad looked up and smiled. "Sorry, it's hard for me to hike and take notes. Thank you for sharing that with me while we summit the highest peak we've been on."

As Chad and Paul reached the summit, they took in the majestic, breathtaking view of the Silver Valley far below. As Grace panted and drank some water Paul had brought for her, Paul reached into his backpack and drew out a small package.

He handed it to Chad, and said, "Chad, God told me that I was not supposed to go on that trip, even though it was something I had planned on and desired for over seventeen years.

"You see, even though I've learned all these things throughout my life, and found success with my company, I've never poured myself into someone like I have with you. When Mrs.B told me about you and the challenges you were experiencing, what needed to happen for you to graduate, I knew I needed to stay."

Tears filled Paul's eyes as he handed Chad his gift. Chad opened the box, and found a silver compass. He lifted the solid metal object, then turned it upside down, where an inscription read, *'To my Son. May God always guide you and direct your path. Love, Paul.'*

Tears of gratitude and joy fell down Chad's cheeks as he stared at the gift, then up at Paul. Chad moved forward and embraced Paul, as only a father and son can. As they turned, the golden sun rose in the sky, signaling a new beginning, a new way of life.

The Beginning ...

Work + Love
Companion Guide:

Below are the 12 principles for finding purpose in your life and work. I encourage you to work through the questions in this guide.

Write your answers down and then read them out loud. There is power in our spoken words, both the power of death and, in the case of this guide, the power of life.

This guide can be used individually or with your team.

Want to go deeper and get personalized support to live these principles out?

Head over to www.MichaelWolsten.com to connect and get free resources to help you on your path.

Who you are matters:
  1. "Who are you and why are you here?"

- Answer this question with absolute honesty. What do you truly believe about this statement?
- Think about your future and what you would like to become. How would you like to answer these questions in the future? What would you like to answer as your future self? What would you say if there were no barriers in your way?
- What differences do you notice between your answers for today and your answers for the future? What role does God play in your answers?

2. How you see the world shapes you:
  "When you look at people through God's eyes, through His lens, you see other people the way that He sees them." ~ Dan Mohler

- The posture and position of your heart, and knowing who you are and whose you are, changes everything.

- How do you see the world? What aggravates you about your personal, day-to-day life? What thoughts, feelings, and emotions should stay, and which ones should go?
- Remember Paul's story of being lost in the Oregon wilderness, all by himself? Have you ever felt or do you currently feel lost on your life's journey? Describe your thoughts.

3. Choosing a Different Path:

- Describe a time you decided to do things on your own, without the wisdom and guidance of others (or maybe in direct opposition to them). How did that go and what did you learn?
- Reread Chapter 4 and put yourself in the place of Chad. How have you displayed the following in your life and work?
- Apathy
- Self-Pity
- Entitlement
- Pride
- Be as specific as possible as you go through your own experiences.

4. A Higher Vision:

- Read Genesis 3:22-23. How does God see you and what does He believe about you?
- "That's the power that God's love has for us: it's uniquely individual and purposeful. He desires a personal relationship with each and every one of us, above everything else, even when we choose to reject him and try to move him out of the way" (from Chapter 5).
- What has God been saying to you throughout your life? What has He been trying to tell you? If an answer does not come to mind right away, please pray and ask for clarity, out loud, until it does.
- Read Colossians 3:22-24. How is God redeeming the work you do and how does this verse tie into what you do each day?

5. Prepare for the Journey:

- What can you accomplish, first thing every morning, to help you be productive and focused?
- "Love carries wisdom with it, and wisdom always carries love. The two are connected, you can't have one without the other." ~ Marilyn Howshall
- When we pray and ask our loving heavenly Father for wisdom, especially out loud, we're activating our faith and making it real. What can you pray for, out loud, and believe for in your work and life?
- Are you a crab (review the story in Chapter 8)? Do you pull others down or lift others up? Are you choosing to spend time with any crabs in your life?
- What is the fruit of your relationships? What do those closest to you experience every day? Do you need to make things right with anyone in your life?

6. Living in Your Strengths:

- What are your natural strengths? What have others said about you or seen in you that you do well, seemingly without trying?
- What did you love to do when you were six? What traits/strengths did you display?
- Complete a Clifton Strengths assessment.
- https://www.gallup.com/cliftonstrengths/en/253850/cliftonstrengths-for-individuals.aspx
- What did it say about you? What did you already know about yourself and what surprised you? Review your strengths with someone who knows you. (They will likely reaffirm what the assessment told you and be able to give you examples.)

7. Your Personal Best:

- What is your personal mission statement? What drives you in your everyday work?

- What is your motivation for growing in your current role?
- What connections have you made so far that tie into your work and life?

8. Apply Like a Spy:

- Who are the leaders and mentors in your life that have helped you along your journey and how can they help you in your current phase of life? What wisdom and resources can they provide?
- What sources do you look at to help you find new opportunities for growth?
- Have you asked questions like the ones in Chapter 11 to help determine if the path you are researching could be a good fit?
- What are your passions and interests? How can you get involved with groups that feel the same way you do about serving or spending their time? What groups exist online or locally that allow you to connect with others?
- Who are the connectors in your life and how can you mutually help each other?

9. Your Best Foot Forward:

- Dress for success! How you look and feel matters. Always dress at least one level higher than you think needed, to show your respect and interest in the opportunity.
- How can you pull your strengths and your story into your communication and make it personal?
- How often do you practice interviews? (either with someone else or videoing yourself)? How can you incorporate this practice into your life? (Be sure to answer the questions in Chapter 12 to help improve your results.)
- As you review your video, be sure to note how you did as far as eye contact, tone, facial expressions, and non-verbal communication, including your smile. :)

- Pray out loud over the process! God is using you for His purposes and refining you! Turn your anxiousness into excitement.

10. Tell Your Story:

- How can you practice your public speaking? Can you send a video to a friend or family member? To a small group or trusted circle of friends? Doing so often will help build your confidence and skills.
- Who is your person? Who can help support you with their words and non-verbal cues as you speak?
- Practice how you Arc and Park. In what ways can you keep your audience engaged and excited about where you are taking them?
- Does your speech or presentation grab the attention of your audience? Is it relevant to them on a deeper level and is it compelling, especially at the end? What will they remember when you are done?
- Where do you want to take your audience, in their hearts and minds? What feelings do you want them to feel and how do you want to change them for the better? Knowing where you want to finish will help you build a presentation that has a lasting impact.

11. Love the Process:

- What areas are you waiting for clarity on? What gives you anxiety when you think about it because you are not sure what the outcome will be?
- What is the path God is leading you on? What can you believe in and stand on in faith, when it comes to your journey?
- Be sure to write down what God is showing you and declare His goodness toward you and for you every day. Share what you believe He is helping you see with a trusted friend, mentor, or family member.

12. Reaching the Mountaintop:

- Remember that there is always another mountain to climb. As you summit, be sure to ask God where He wants to take you next.
- Take time to look back at the valleys, the low points, and your progress along the way. What did you learn that you want to make sure you do again and what things will you not do again? The mountaintops help give us perspective and vision for more.
- Invest in others. Who can benefit from your story and progress? How can you help others walk the path they were meant to walk?

Discover even more resources at MichaelWolsten.com

ABOUT THE AUTHORS

Above all else, I am a husband to my beautiful wife, father to my incredible three boys, and son of our Heavenly Father, the best dad anyone could have. Some of my story is shared with you throughout this book.

I worked in college as a laundry sorter. I was the prideful young professional who left a good job for the wrong commission-only job and almost lost our home in the process. I know what it is like to be in the forefront and feeling like I was faking it. I was the one who almost didn't graduate from college.

My twenty-year career is a combination of mistakes, triumphs, failures, learning, and now teaching and mentoring. I have taken everything I have learned through my life, as a Vice President for one of the nation's largest credit unions and running my consulting practice to see the tangible success of depositing into the lives of others. I can now speak to groups of hundreds or one-on-one with authenticity, because I firmly believe I am becoming who I was created to be. I now get to help leaders find their own path through my courses and executive coaching to create breakthroughs that can change everything.

I am on a mission to empower those around me to be the best version of themselves. To bring out the gifts, strengths, and good stuff that God has put in each of us. Going through this process with my own boys helped shape this book and I am grateful to learn from them as they grow into world changers.

My son Henry has always loved stories, as long as I can remember. His bouncy excitement and love for life are on display for those who know him and his voice is evident throughout this book. He has a heart for God and is walking the path that few dare to walk on. I feel privileged to be his father. We live in Coeur d'Alene, Idaho and enjoy the beauty we are surrounded by all year long. We are playing on the lake in the summer, hiking at many of the spots highlighted in this book, and skiing together in the winter.

Lead Courageously,
Michael

~

To connect with me personally:
Info@MichaelWolsten.com
MichaelWolsten.com
Thank You's

This book would not be possible without my wife Kelly, the love of my life. Your encouragement means so much to me!

To AJ, there are no words to describe your impact on this project and on me. Love you brother!

To Ann Tatlock, I am in awe of your editing talents and ability to help my story come to life.

To my son Henry, I love you and there is no way this book would have happened without your love for story and dedication. Our months full of work paid off, even if we did have to listen to Vibin' Cat Polka on repeat to make it happen. :)

To my parents, Paul and Sharon, who have always shown me what hard work and dedication look like. Love you so much!

To Gail and Vance, your consistent love and encouragement, even when I had no idea who I really was, will always stay with me. Thank you for letting me marry your beautiful daughter.

To Bill and Bernie, I want to be like you when I grow up. What a legacy of love you have left for us and the lessons you taught us way back when will never be forgotten.

To Marilyn Howshall, who has shown me and my family what love really means and how to live a life full of good fruit. I am forever grateful.

To John and Michelle, you both have a special place in our family's heart and I am so thankful for all your help!

To my boys, you are the reason I wrote this book. Oliver, Henry, and Elliot your hearts and impact on this life will be determined by your relationships and I am so proud of the men you are becoming. You each will bring so much to your families, to the workplace, and to our world through your character and love. I can't wait to watch you implement these principles in your work and live a life few dare to dream of. Love you my dudes!

Thank you to everyone listed below. You played a role in conversations that lead to this book happening!

Russ and Hollie Johnson, Daniel Johnson, Noah Marshall, Matt Buonocore, Michelle Ekert, Mark Kunz, Dustin Patchen, Aydan Salois, Josh Hebert, Daniel Gephart, Corey Dahle, Meg Calvin, Derek Murphy and Jonathan Heston!

One Last Thing... If you enjoyed this book and found it useful, it would mean the world to me if you would take 5 minutes and post a short review on Amazon. Your support really makes a huge difference, and I read every single review, so I can get your feedback and make this book even better!

If you'd like to leave a review, all you need to do is use this link to head to this book's Amazon page here:

Thank you for walking your path to purpose.

Made in the USA
Monee, IL
01 June 2023